LAMAN LIBRARY

5705 7

D1309965

J
Carlson
Chalou.

3

DISCARD
THIS BOOK IS NO LONGER
THE PROPERTY OF THE
WILLIAM F. LAMAN PUBLIC LIBRARY

WM. F. LAMAN PUBLIC LIBRARY
CIVIC CENTER
NORTH LITTLE ROCK. ARKANSAS

ARGENTA BRANCH LIBRARY

WM. F. LAMAN PUBLIC LIBRARY
CIVIC CENTER
NORTH LITTLE ROCK. ARKANSAS

OTHER BOOKS BY NATALIE SAVAGE CARLSON

A Brother for the Orphelines

Carnival in Paris

The Empty Schoolhouse

The Family Under the Bridge

The Happy Orpheline

Jean-Claude's Island

The Letter on the Tree

The Orphelines in the Enchanted Castle

A Pet for the Orphelines

Sailor's Choice

Sashes Red and Blue

The Song of the Lop-Eared Mule

The Talking Cat

The Tomahawk Family

Wings Against the Wind

CHALOU

HARPER & ROW, PUBLISHERS
New York, Evanston, and London

CHALOU

by

Natalie Savage Carlson

WILLIAM F. LAMAN PUBLIC LIBRARY
ARGENTA BRANCH LIBRARY
506 MAIN STREET
NORTH LITTLE ROCK, AR 72114

Pictures by George Loh

WM. F. LAMAN PUBLIC LIBRARY
CIVIC CENTER
NORTH LITTLE ROCK, ARKANSAS

82663

CHALOU

Text copyright © 1967 by Natalie Savage Carlson
Pictures copyright © 1967 by George Loh

Printed in the United States of America. All rights reserved.
No part of this book may be used or reproduced in any manner whatsoever without written permission except in the
case of brief quotations embodied in critical articles and re-
views. For information address Harper & Row, Publishers,
Incorporated, 49 East 33rd Street, New York, N.Y. 10016.

Library of Congress Catalog Card Number: AC 67–10034

For my daughter, Julie,
who used selections from the original
manuscript in her Master's thesis
for the University of Rhode Island

CONTENTS

CHALOU

THE DAIRY FARM

1

In winter the St. Lawrence River moves in a granite channel overlapped by enamel-like shelves of ice and snow. And the French-Canadian farms and villages on its shores are buried under a white blanket.

On Ernest Pinard's dairy farm, not far from the city of Quebec, the cattle were penned in the big red barn day after day.

Chalou, the big guard dog, was freed from his duty of watching over the herd in the river pasture. He was a tawny brindle dog with a long black muzzle and clubbed black paws—of the build favored by farmers of that region. He was as fierce with enemies of the livestock as he was gentle with members of the family and the farm animals.

In the winter, with the fields and the cattle resting, he was free to play with the Pinard boys. He had begun waiting for their school bus at the end of the lane each afternoon.

One day the boys swung off the bus full of their own feeling of freedom after the restrictions of the high school rooms in Ste. Odile.

"Let's get the toboggan out and slide down the river bank," Remi suggested as their boots crunched through the ruts in the lane.

"I have some math problems to do," answered the younger Jean, "and I want to get to work on them while they're still fresh in my mind."

"Oh, what a great scholar you are!" scoffed Remi. "I'm glad my school days will be over when I graduate this year. But come on, little brother. You have all evening for lessons, and daylight won't last much longer."

Already twilight was beginning to spread a crayon blue smear on both shores of the river.

"For just a couple slides," Jean agreed. "Then you can keep on by yourself, because I want to get my problems done before milking time."

Jean was a square-faced youth of fifteen with his father's blond hair and blue eyes. Ernest Pinard would often introduce him to strangers, saying, "This is my younger son, but it is he who will carry on with the farm and the herd when I am gone."

On the other hand, he usually said, "And this is Remi. Older sons are different from what they were in the days of our

2

fathers. This one already plans to go away to work on the north shore of the gulf."

The older boy had inherited his mother's black hair and eyes, but his love of change and adventure was his own. His friend Fabien Tremblay was already working at the titanium ore terminal near Havre St. Pierre. He wrote glowing reports about the big pay connected with driving one of the mobile cranes.

"I now own a big fine automobile," he wrote. "One gets rich fast here."

But Remi would have to work in the village part of the summer to make enough money for the trip and for expenses while he was looking for his high-paying job.

Despite their difference in appearance and character, the Pinard boys had a strong affection for each other and were usually to be found together. It might have been because they were the only offspring of the Pinard couple.

They climbed the hill toward the old farmhouse with the tips of its roof curved to keep the snow from falling close to the walls and windows. It was so cold that they could walk up the hard crust of the snow to fling their book bags on the porch.

Remi got the toboggan from the nearby shed. Then they followed the cleared path that climbed the brow of the bluff. Chalou trailed behind, wagging his plumy tail.

On the way they passed the old outdoor oven. The snow-shingled roof covering the clay was slatted by a few remaining boards. The snow reached up to its rusted door hanging on one hinge. Once the cat had had kittens in it and sometimes the chickens roosted on top, but it was never used for baking anymore because Madame Pinard bought her bread at the store.

Chalou ran to the oven and sniffed inside because it was often a haven for field mice. But its blackened cavern was empty, so he trotted on to rejoin the boys.

At the top of the long slippery incline to the ice sheath on the river they stopped. Below them were the frozen banks with the little fishing cabin out on the rough ice. The haze had deepened to azure on the shores of the St. Lawrence.

"It's your turn to sit in front," said Jean as Remi maneuvered the toboggan into position. "I was there last time."

The boys kept strict account of such things.

Chalou began running around on the snow and barking excitedly. He nipped at Remi's boot first then at Jean's plaid jacket.

"Oh, let's put Chalou in front," suggested Remi.

So the older boy sat in the middle, bracing Chalou between his legs. Jean gave the toboggan a strong shove, then jumped on behind. They began careening down the hill. Too late Remi found out that with the dog in front he was unable to steer. The toboggan raced down the hill, struck an outcropping row, and swerved to the left. It threatened to upset them, then took a dizzy curve and went over the steeper cliff on the other side. Gaining speed, it rushed madly toward a fir tree near the bottom and crashed into the trunk.

Jean slid off the side and Remi was tossed into a snowdrift. Chalou, in front, took the brunt of the impact. His body was

4

flung against the tree and only his long shaggy hair kept him from injury.

The boys sat in the snow and laughed uproariously. Chalou pulled himself together with a disconcerted look.

"Poor Chalou!" said Jean. "He looks as if he thinks it was all his fault."

"It was," answered Remi breathlessly, "because he was in front and didn't steer straight."

"We'll put him in back next time," suggested Jean.

But there was no next time for the dog. No matter how much they coaxed him, he would not come within arm's reach of either of the boys, and he wouldn't go anywhere near the toboggan. He waited until they began coasting without him, then he chased them down, barking and skidding over the smooth surface.

At the bottom Remi paused to break the ice crust and scoop his hands full of snow. He molded it into a tight ball.

"Here, Chalou, boy," he cried. "Catch!"

He tossed the snowball into the air. Chalou eagerly went after it. It missed his nose and disintegrated near his paws.

Chalou began scratching through the crust in search of the ball. The boys again laughed heartily. Remi repeated the performance and again Chalou tried to find the ball in the snow. He was puzzled by its mysterious disappearance. Then he neatly caught one of the balls, but as his teeth bit into it, it went to pieces and covered his face with a white mask.

Chalou had learned about the cold white balls, too. He refused to chase any more of them.

6

"Chalou's finished and so am I," stated Jean. "I'm going back to the house."

In the kitchen that evening the boys told their parents about their sport on the river bank and Chalou's part in it.

"You should have seen him with the snow all over his face," said Remi, chuckling. "He looked like Good Man Winter at the carnival in Quebec."

Madame Pinard was not too amused.

"You will spoil that dog," she warned as she ladled the pea soup. "He will be no more good as a guard dog. He will want to be playing with you boys instead of watching the cattle. Last year he had the little heifer to keep his mind on his work. But she has grown up now, so what about this spring when the cows return to the pasture?"

Jean looked worried at this, but his father calmed his fears.

"Chalou is a well-trained dog," he said. "I promise you that he will never forget his duty. Let him have some fun with the boys while he can."

THE FISHING CABIN

2

In the spring the shelves of ice along the borders of the St. Lawrence begin breaking up. Great chunks of it move down the river in a widening trough. The *suroît,* the wind of the south, speeds them to their watery doom.

On the Pinard farm the paths through the snow were melting into slush. The icicles hanging from the eaves of the house and the floor of the porch were dripping like leaky faucets, and small avalanches kept sliding from the roof of the big red barn.

The cattle, after having been penned in the barn most of the winter, welcomed their new freedom in the barnyard. They trod the snow into a brown mush and tossed their horns with fresh vigor.

One Saturday morning Ernest Pinard was beginning his routine of milking the cows with Chalou at his heels. He fitted the suction cups of the milking machines to the cows' udders. When he turned on the switch, a loud hum punctuated by the pulsating clicks of the pump filled the air.

Even as Chalou was typical of the farm dogs in Quebec province, Ernest Pinard had the looks of the farmers found there. He was a thin man with deep-set blue eyes, and shoulders bent forward from long hours with the pitchfork and the plow. Hard labor had strengthened his muscles into wire rather than rope.

"It is spring, Chalou," he said to the dog, who always slept in the barn during the night. "I told you that winter would not last forever." He rolled his eyes to the dwindling pile of hay in the loft above. "But neither does last year's hay. We will soon have to get to work in the fields."

The big dog seemed to understand the man's words. He put his nose against a crack in the barn door and sniffed. Then he went to the free stall where Bichette and the other heifers still strangers to the sucking machines were feeding from the manger.

He was especially devoted to the doe-eyed Jersey. He had been present at the hard birth which had claimed her mother's life. He had lain whimpering in the hay, shamed by his failure to protect one of the herd from a danger against which his fangs were powerless. But he had quickly adopted the newborn calf, fostering her through her first frail months and guarding her when she grew into a graceful heifer.

Chalou went alongside her and nuzzled her yellow throat.

9

Bichette stopped eating long enough to lower her head and run her moist nose across his muzzle.

The dog trotted back to the milk cows in their stanchions. Most of them were fawn-and-white Guernseys quite used to the mechanical tug of the suction cups.

When the cows were freed from the long hoses, the farmer opened the stable door and set them loose in the barnyard. They gathered in a sunny corner, chewing their cuds and enjoying the spring sunshine on their heads and backs. Bichette rested her neck across that of one of the Guernseys.

Chalou seemed satisfied that all was well with the herd. He went loping off to find the Pinard boys, but they had left early to drive their mother into town for the weekly shopping.

So the dog made a dutiful round of the henhouse and the pigpen. Then he followed the boundaries of the farm, passing the earthen wall topped with great boulders that formed one side of the pasture. He jumped up on it and surveyed the ragged blanket of snow covering the cattle's summer forage.

When the boys returned from town, they had school work to do. Chalou had to wait until late afternoon for their company.

"Why don't we get in some more fishing before the ice shelf melts?" suggested Remi to his brother as he shoved his books and papers into a disorderly heap. "Papa has been talking about dragging the cabin back on land."

"I'm sure the little tomcod are gone," said Jean, carefully packing his school work into the bag so it would be ready for Monday morning. "And the ice isn't safe now."

10

"We might catch something else," persisted Remi. "Come on, Jean. Be a good sport."

The younger boy shrugged his shoulders. "We won't catch anything," he insisted, "but I'll go with you. I'd like a breath of fresh air."

They put on the winter jackets that wouldn't be needed much longer.

Chalou was waiting for them on the back steps. The boys trudged down the muddy path with him following at their heels. They walked through the fringe of firs and down the bare bank.

They headed for the little cabin perched near the open channel. It had been a chicken house, but their father had added runners and a stovepipe chimney, and the boys had proudly painted it red. Each winter it was pulled out on the ice by the tractor.

The channel had nibbled closer to the cabin. Already dark streaks of faulty ice were noticeable.

"*Tata!*" exclaimed Jean. "We'd better not stay here. And we must tell Papa to hurry with the cabin."

"Oh, come on," urged Remi. "We won't stay long. It's our last chance to do any fishing through the ice. We can tell Papa about it when we go back with some fish."

Jean looked dubious, but Remi boldly hurried on to the cabin. Chalou whined a little as he crossed the dark shadows, but where the boys went he would go too.

Although the cabin was floorless, an attempt at comfort had

12

been made. A faded hooked rug covered part of the cold ice. There were boxes to sit on. A bench piled with threadbare blankets would accommodate any hardy enthusiast who wished to spend the night. And the little stove in the corner promised that one might keep warm as long as the stack of firewood behind it lasted.

On the other side yawned an open hole axed in the surface by Remi and Jean. It was their fishing pool.

Remi pulled out the jar of old fish morsels still half-frozen and selected one that was mostly fin. He was eager to see what fish might be hungry. He seated himself on a box and baited his hook with the fin. He lowered the line into the water while Jean was trying to start a fire in the stove.

When the dry sticks began snapping, Jean fixed himself a line and joined his brother at the edge of the hole.

"Bite, bite, little fishes," sang Remi, trying to cast an old fisherman's spell. But it did not work. The tomcod were gone and the other fish too sluggish from the cold water to be interested. "Let's set a tip-up for Chalou to watch while we go skating," he suggested. "Perhaps we can catch a big sturgeon."

"All right." Jean was ready to agree. "The skating won't last much longer either."

Remi quickly abandoned his line and pulled a pair of skate shoes from one of the boxes. The boys found it handy to keep them in the cabin.

Jean fastened his line to a piece of wire tied with a flag of red cloth. The wire was bent into a hoop and its end slipped into a

13

hook. A tug on the line would trip the hook, springing up the flag.

He got his own skates and began slipping off his boots. Half of his attention was hopefully turned to the tip-up, but the flag remained dipped.

The boys rose, Remi first, and skated out. They left the door open. The dog would have followed them, but he was ordered back.

"You watch the tip-up," commanded Jean.

That was one of Chalou's tricks which delighted the boys. When the flag flew up, Chalou would bark excitedly, then run outside to tug at a trouser leg until its wearer hurried to land the fish. Remi had even tried to think of some way to teach the dog to pull the line up by himself.

This time Chalou was not willing to stay. Jean had to order him back three times, and Remi finally emphasized it with a slap at his muzzle.

The dog watched the boys skim away on winged feet. He whined some more.

Then he settled down to wait at the edge of the fishing hole. He even stretched his nose over it and tried to pierce the depths for sight of a fish.

He waited a long time with a patience unknown to his masters. Already they had forgotten the tip-up and were racing farther and farther away.

Finally Chalou grew bored. He stretched his body over the hooked rug and closed his eyes.

14

Meanwhile the tide from the far-off ocean rose and so did the cold wind. Wind and tide joined forces against the current. The water heaved under the ice. The cabin shook. Then there was an explosive blast as though from a hunter's rifle.

The floor lurched. The tip-up sprang, its red flag violently quivering as if a mighty sturgeon had seized the hook. Chalou jumped to his paws with a frightened yelp. He stood trembling with indecision at such an unexpected attack from an invisible enemy.

Water from the hole splashed over the hooked rug and wet his clubby paws. The cabin careened crazily. The door swung wildly on its hinges. Chalou leaped through it before it swung shut with a finality that would have trapped him inside.

Outside a dark fissure in the ice was widening. The upheaval had cracked loose the slab on which the cabin sat. The dog crouched and tightened his steely muscles to spring across the open water to the shore ice, but it was too late. He was already too far from the opposite edge. In the distance the figures of the boys were indistinguishable from those of the low firs that staked the shoreline.

Chalou let out a volley of staccato barks. As the ice floe carrying him and the cabin drifted farther from land, his frenzy grew. He was a good swimmer and might have set out for the shore, but the rough water was clattering loose ice all around him. He ran in circles, barking for help.

The fingers of a strong eddy reached for the floe. They gave it a twirl, which drew the dog's claws deep into the ice and

15

loosened the runners of the cabin. Then the floe steadied as it was drawn down the river.

Chalou was overcome with despair at his precarious position. He raised his black muzzle into the wind and howled like a werewolf.

THE ICEBREAKER

3

Next day the icebreaker *Frontenac* of the Canadian Coast Guard left Quebec, her course set for the Labrador Sea, where ice still threatened shipping and the sealing operations.

A crowd of friends and relatives of the crew had gathered on the dock to bid them farewell. Even a dog was present to see his master off. He sat high on the giant stump of a dock bollard, the better to look over the waving handkerchiefs of the milling throng.

The crewmen crowded the decks and waved their caps. Among them stood Pierre Laforge, a dark young man with a square jaw and square shoulders. He was the descendant of generations of French-Canadian pilots who had sailed boats on the St. Lawrence.

As the *Frontenac* slipped into the stream, the mournful howls of the pointer rose above the cries of the people on shore. The men on the icebreaker laughed.

"Even the dog is brokenhearted to see us leave," said one of them.

"It is my dog," Pierre proudly explained. "He seems to understand even better than my little son that I will be gone for a long time." He waved his cap in great arcs. "*Au revoir*, Mickie," he shouted. "Be a good dog and take care of Mama and Jeannot until I return."

The crowd on the dock and the dog on the bollard faded into the distance as the *Frontenac*'s sturdy red bow ploughed through the gray water. Her squat smokestack, painted with a red maple leaf, rose above her white superstructure.

Soon even the landmarks of Quebec had disappeared. The medieval Chateau Frontenac on its great rock and the old town below faded into the gallery of clouds that had gathered over the shoreline.

"The St. Lawrence has opened well," said Captain Brignac to the man at the wheel in the pilothouse. He raked his binoculars across the choppy water. "The batture ice is breaking up from the shore now."

The chief officer joined them, the hood of his parka flung back over his shoulders. Both he and his captain were veterans of arctic waters.

"Excuse me, sir," he announced, "but the lookout aloft reports some kind of an animal on a floe about ten miles to starboard. He thinks it is a wolf."

"What does he expect me to do?" snapped the captain. "Capture it for the Quebec Zoo?"

"No, sir," answered the other, "but he also thinks it might be a dog."

Captain Brignac reached across the empty coffee mugs on the table for the chart.

"It will take us off course," he growled, "but we shall investigate. If it's a wolf, bad luck for him and us too, because we've wasted time."

"And if it's a dog?" queried the watch officer.

The tight lines around the captain's lips relaxed. "If it's a dog," he answered, "we will close in and lower a man on the Jacob's ladder." The ends of his lips raised in a smile. "Perhaps it is the dog that stole the show when we left Quebec."

Chalou had quieted down after a long vigil of mournful howling. Since it appeared that Remi and Jean could not come to rescue him, he had begun seeking his own means of escape.

He circled the slab of ice numberless times. He was surrounded by dark forbidding water and the other floes that bobbed past him. And now he was too far from shore to swim for it.

Night closed in early on the St. Lawrence valley and the lighthouses along the coasts began to twinkle like fireflies. Then the darkness was brightened by a spectral glow to the north—the beginning of the dance of the marionettes, as it was called by the old woodsmen. The pink and green northern lights flickered across the backdrop of black sky. Chalou's dark form could have been that of a wolf crouching on arctic ice. He dozed fitfully. He trembled in his sleep and his nose twitched.

When dawn came in the east, the dog began treading the edge of the floe again.

A jagged cake of ice lurched at it. The cabin was jarred loose from its ruts, and it went sliding toward the edge. Chalou's claws chiseled angular scrawls as he sought to balance himself. For a moment the little shed clung, then it slid off into the river. For several yards it floated upside down.

It began sinking slowly, until Chalou, looking down, could see the boxes and the bench flung against the stove that now rested on the roof. The hooked rug and the blankets were awash. The fishing line, its end snagged by a nail, stretched far behind as if trolling for salmon. Soon there was nothing afloat except the boxes and the bench. They became lost in the brash ice.

As the river widened, the ice chunks spread apart. For a while Chalou rode as comfortably as if he were in Madame Pinard's rocking chair.

Then he saw an encouraging sight. A great red hulk was moving toward him. He could see the figures of men on its deck.

As the ship drew closer Chalou began making desperate little moves as if to leap into the river to swim to her. He was held back only by his compulsion to tighten his throat and howl his appeals for help.

As the *Frontenac* closed in on him, the dog became frantic with joy. He jumped up and down, quivering with anticipation and impatience. He twirled and danced on his hind legs.

ARGENTA BRANCH LIBRARY

WM. F. LAMAN PUBLIC LIBRARY
CIVIC CENTER
NORTH LITTLE ROCK, ARKANSAS

82663

From the bridge the first officer conned the ship to the speed and drift of the ice floe. A Jacob's ladder was lowered from the fantail.

"Now who will volunteer to go down and get the dog?" asked the chief officer.

A gaunt seaman from the Labrador coast shook his head. "Not me," he said. "I've seen those Eskimo huskies tear a man to pieces when he slipped and fell among them."

"He may be unmanageable even if he's friendly," said an Acadian, who spoke his French with a quaint accent. "And I don't like his size."

But Pierre Laforge stepped forward with alacrity. "I'll fetch him," he offered. "I always get along well with dogs."

The others watched as Laforge slipped down the ladder. Scarcely had his feet touched the floe than Chalou hurled all of his weight on him. The man was knocked down by the dog's gratitude. Chalou planted his paws against Laforge's shoulders and licked his face.

Those above guffawed heartily now that their moment of anxiety was over.

"Hand him a bone, Pierre, before he starts gnawing on you," cried one.

"He's only getting along well with you," added another.

"Bravo, dog," shouted a third. "You win the match."

Pierre had to fight off Chalou's affection before he could rise to his feet. The dog continued his capers, but they subsided as the man calmly patted him and spoke in a low, encouraging tone.

23

A rope was dropped over the side, and Pierre looped it securely around the dog's quivering body. Then Chalou was drawn up through the air, twirling and barking.

Now that it had been proven that he was not vicious, strong arms were willing to pull him over the side. He was released from the rope.

A towering figure came striding down the deck. Chalou raced to him and began jumping against him.

"Down, fellow!" ordered Captain Brignac. "Down, I say!"

He grabbed the dog by the scruff of the neck and forced him against the deck. Chalou recognized the note of command in the voice and kept his place.

The captain fingered the long hair at the dog's throat.

"He has no collar or identification tag," he said, "so unfortunately we cannot see that he is returned to anyone. He will have to be turned over to the dog constable when we put into port."

"I'll take charge of him, sir," Laforge volunteered again.

The captain smiled at him. "I seem to remember that you left a dog behind in Quebec."

"Yes, sir," admitted Laforge. "I know he'd like to be in this one's place right now." Knowing dogs as he did, the man added, "I will take him to the galley right away. He must be hungry if he's been on that floe very long. Come, Loup—Wolf," he ordered. "That's as good a name for you as any because they thought you were a wolf at first."

Chalou's ears recognized the Loup as part of his name. He wagged his plumed tail. He followed Pierre across the deck and into a companionway.

At the top of the steep hatchway the man hesitated. "This is going to be another problem," he said.

A tantalizing aroma was coming from below. It had the ingredients of Madame Pinard's supper soup with its minced onions, cubed potatoes, yellow peas and just a touch of garlic.

Chalou turned around and began backing down the hatchway in the manner he used on the ladder in the Pinard barn. One hind paw after the other reached for a lower step while each front paw took its turn clinging to a higher one.

Pierre was filled with admiration. "You could have come up the Jacob's ladder with me," he stated.

The galley was a long, narrow room with an oil-fired range and great steam kettles. The cook stood at a work table peeling more onions for the stew. He looked at the dog through stinging tears.

"Another mouth to feed," he remarked glumly. "And they didn't deliver all the supplies we requested in Quebec."

"Fry him up some eggs," suggested Pierre.

"We're running out of lard, too," added the cook. But he spooned a generous chunk of it into a skillet and began cracking eggs.

When he went to the cupboard to get a deep bowl, Pierre quickly added two more eggs to those in the skillet.

In the Gulf

4

After the rocking and tossing of the ice floe, the heavy roll of the *Frontenac*'s round bottom did not disturb Chalou. The decks and companionways soon became familiar. He could go from the fantail to the fo'c's'le deck as easily as he had found his way from the south pasture to the Pinard barn.

But it was the crew's quarters that he preferred. He had quickly become a favorite with the men. There was always a relaxed, comfortable air about the room where they gathered to chat or play cards.

"He must be a farm dog," said the young man from the south shore, looking up from his game of bluff. "They have dogs like him back home. They are good watchdogs for the farmers."

"In my young day you used to see such dogs pulling little

wagons," reminisced the man from the Gaspé who sat across from him. "A dog worked for his keep in those days."

"Not like these city dogs," agreed another. "Do you know that my wife wants a toy poodle?" He raised his voice to a high falsetto to imitate a woman. " 'Please buy me a dear little poodle, Eustache, to take your place when you are gone.' It was an insult, so I refused to buy the poodle."

"A dog should be good for something," agreed Pierre Laforge. "My Mickie is the best hunting dog in the province, I can tell you. But I so seldom get leave during hunting season. It is an injustice to the dog."

"My family have forgotten what I look like," said the Acadian from Nova Scotia. "I keep asking myself why I chose the Coast Guard when I am so fond of my home."

"Probably for the same reason I keep re-enlisting," said the Gaspé man. "When I am out on a cruise like this, I am homesick for my wife and little ones. Then when I am home with them, I grow restless. The ocean tide gets into a sailor's blood. It draws him ashore, then pulls him back to sea."

As they talked together the radio operator appeared in the doorway and joined them.

"Loaf and play while you can," he announced cheerlessly. "We just got a message from Ice Operations that the ore carrier *Titania* is icebound near the Strait of Belle Isle. So it's back to work, my hearty boys."

Later, when Chalou went out on deck, the expanse of water was much wider, and the cold wind blowing up the river smelled of the salty sea and the evergreen forests. It carried no

27

familiar odor of cattle and hay and plowed earth.

"We'll get to the ice any day now," Pierre said to Chalou after they had passed Anticosti, the island which lay like a bone at the throat of the gulf. "Do you want to ride on it again?"

They entered the icefields the very next day. It was as if time had turned back to winter again. Land and water were glazed with a rough white frosting.

"Not too bad yet," stated the Labrador man. "We can follow the old channel cut by the last icebreaker through."

The channel was not much wider than the beam of the *Frontenac*. The officers and men were doubly alert now. Chalou received less attention.

"The wind and tide are drifting the icefield and the channel," remarked Captain Brignac as he looked through his binoculars.

"That is probably what trapped the *Titania*," suggested his watch officer.

The *Frontenac* shoved through the newly formed ice, pushing the old pans apart. Her prow cracked through the more stubborn ones. At last they reached the beleaguered carrier. Chalou was on deck with his paws on the railing. He was intently watching the figures of the men on the *Titania*. Perhaps Remi and Jean were among them.

An icebreaker is equipped with a raised reinforced bow. When the *Frontenac* was driven upon the ice, her weight and surge crushed it. As she approached the carrier's bow head-on, great circular cracks spread over the ice.

The ship pitched and shuddered as she broke through. Chalou jumped back from the railing and tried to dig his claws into the wood of the deck.

The men laughed at the dog's fright.

"What's the matter, Loup?" asked the young man from the south shore. "You should be used to this—the way you rode that floe."

The man from Labrador said, "I tell you I'd rather be shook up on the *Frontenac* than froze in solid on the *Titania*."

The icebreaker circled the freighter to cut her loose, then she sailed back into her original channel. Slowly the *Titania* followed.

"We will lead her into port because she's having trouble with her rudder," said the captain to the chief officer. "We can tie up long enough to take on more provisions. And that will give us a chance to put the dog ashore too."

The men off duty rested in their quarters after their big job was over. Chalou lay on the deck at Pierre Laforge's feet.

"They say the captain is going to hand Loup over to the authorities in Havre St. Pierre," announced the south shore man, who had just come off of watch.

The crewmen were aghast at this news.

"I would take him home myself," said Pierre, "but Mickie would not stand for it. He is a jealous dog."

"My family would take him," said the man from Labrador, "but those Eskimo dogs would tear him to pieces."

"He is a splendid beast," admitted the young man from the south shore, "but I live with my family on a farm and they

already have two dogs, five cats, and my mother's canary."

"And he is just what I would choose to take my place at home," said Eustache, "but my wife has put her heart on a toy poodle. She would lock both of us out of the apartment."

Then the inspiration came to Pierre Laforge. "It is very simple," he explained. "We all want Loup but none of us can take him home. So we ask the captain if we may keep him on the ship as our mascot."

"Just the right idea," agreed the Labrador man. "I wonder I didn't think of it myself."

The captain readily agreed to their request.

"It will be good for their morale while they are on this dreary mission," he said to his chief officer. "And I really wouldn't feel right in turning the dog over to the authorities. They probably would destroy him."

It was noon when the icebreaker approached the harbor of Havre St. Pierre. It was set in a deep cove with its waters protected by Anticosti Island.

The Coast Guard ship left her charge at the ore terminal, then moored at a large dock near the sandy beach.

Amid the shouts of the crew, the thumping of ropes, the clank of metal, and scuttling footsteps Chalou managed to stay out of the way.

Then he went to where the gangway was being laid. He smelled land and houses and smoke. He also smelled winter because it was reluctant to depart from this area of Canada. A crochet of snow netted the landscape.

Chalou was eager for the familiar feel of earth under his paws. He bounded down the gangway.

The officer of the deck called after him, "Do you have permission to go ashore, Loup?" Then as the dog started down the dock, he called, "You better be back by sailing time or you'll get left behind."

Chalou hesitated near the end of the dock. Fringes of snow bordered the road that led up to the town. But the compass in his head told him that his way lay along the river's bank.

32

He passed dock workers and parked trucks. He leaped to the beach and began following it westward. He slipped over a rough cuticle of stubborn ice and trotted across the cold sand.

After some miles the Romaine River, flowing into the St. Lawrence, blocked his way. He followed it to a narrow elbow across which he could swim. He gingerly waded out, his claws scratching and dislodging the small rocks under the water.

He plunged into the frigid current and began paddling, his head held high. For many yards he fought the current until his claws scraped against rocks again. He slowly pulled himself out, cold and dripping, upon the narrow rocky beach crowded by a line of spruce trees.

When he finally reached a cluster of houses, a bristly dog with a snipey nose came snarling toward him and barred his way.

Although the dog was much smaller than he, Chalou could appreciate his property rights. Many times he himself had challenged strange dogs trespassing on the Pinard farm. He turned away. The dog followed him suspiciously for a while and growled for him to be off at greater speed.

So Chalou headed for an open field beyond the houses. It was the summer camping ground of a Montagnais tribe, deserted now because the Indians had gone to their trapping grounds in the Far North.

The dog continued on a graveled road that led westward with invitation and promise, although there were more small rivers to swim.

THE FISHING VILLAGE

5

The next day Chalou reached Rivière au Tonnerre, a fishing village gathered loosely at the mouth of a river. By this time hunger was twisting a sharp blade in his belly. When he came to a scatter of buildings standing bleakly on a treeless plain, he was encouraged because no dogs came to drive him away.

A boy and a girl were walking down the road. They were swinging lunch pails on their arms and both wore heavy rubber boots. Chalou trotted faster toward them. He bounded to the boy and smelled at his lunch pail. His nose told him that there was a pork sandwich inside.

The children were surprised to encounter the friendly dog.

"I've never seen him here before," said the boy. "I wonder where he came from."

He was a sturdy boy around ten years of age with large gray eyes. His knit cap was tucked into the pocket of his plaid jacket, and the breeze riffled his straight hair.

"Here, big doggie!" invited the little girl. "Come to Fleur-Ange."

It was easy to see that she was the boy's younger sister. She had his large gray eyes, but her own hair was curly under her red cap.

The dog moved over to her and she patted his head. Chalou smelled the lunch pail and learned that it contained the same contents as that of the boy.

"He's hungry," said Fleur-Ange. "I'm going to give him a piece of my sandwich."

"You'll be sorry at lunch recess," said the boy, "and you'll beg for some of mine, but I won't give it to you."

The girl paid no attention to him. She opened her pail and with great deliberation tore off half of a half of a sandwich.

Chalou gulped it so fast that for a moment she thought perhaps it had dropped on the ground instead of his tongue. He began whimpering for more.

"He must be starved, Joseph," said the girl. "Why don't you give him some of your sandwich? You ate a big breakfast."

"I'm saving mine for lunch," retorted Joseph.

The girl gave Chalou the rest of her sandwich half. And he still seemed so hungry that she sighed and fed him the other half. After some serious thought, because she loved blueberry pie, she gave him her wedge of it.

"You'll have to go without lunch," the boy reminded her. "You've wasted it on an old stray dog."

Seeing that all of Fleur-Ange's food was gone except for an apple, which he did not relish, Chalou began pestering Joseph.

"Oh, all right," the boy said reluctantly. "I'll give you the crusts off my sandwich. I don't like them anyhow."

He grudgingly tore the crusts from the bread and fed them to the dog.

Some other children on their way to school joined Fleur-Ange and Joseph.

"Is that your dog?" asked one. "I didn't know you had one."

"Where did you get him?" asked another enviously. "I wish I had a big dog like that."

They all gathered around the strange dog. Chalou returned their interest. He hadn't been around children for a long time.

Joseph shook his head. "He's some old stray dog and he's eating up all our lunches. Now Fleur-Ange won't have anything at noon but an apple."

The new arrivals wanted to see Chalou perform at eating school lunches. One after another found a tidbit in his lunch to give the dog—a cold wiener, some potato chips, a crust torn from a sandwich.

The school bell rang.

Fleur-Ange put down her lunch pail and gave Chalou a big hug. She rubbed her cheek against his muzzle.

"Come with me," she invited him. "If you'll wait outside, I'll take you home with us and see that you get a good meal tonight."

The promise meant nothing to Chalou's ears, but he had never known the affection of a little girl. The Pinard boys had given him friendly thumps or had patted his head, but they never had hugged him so tenderly.

The children splashed through the mud, waving their lunch pails as they raced for the open gate of the little schoolhouse. Chalou followed them.

"Now you be sure to wait," repeated Fleur-Ange.

Chalou ran his nose along her wrist, inviting her to hug him again. Fleur-Ange gave him a tight squeeze, then tickled his ear.

Chalou would have followed her right inside the school, but a stern older boy slammed the door in his face. So he waited outside the peaked entrance to the building.

He waited until recess, then played tag with the children in the wet weeds of the schoolyard until an older boy, at the teacher's order, led him back to the road and closed the gate of the slatted fence.

Chalou stayed at the gate until that afternoon when school was dismissed. He followed Joseph and Fleur-Ange to their home, a bleak gray house with a blue roof that was separated from the road by a broken rail fence. Tepees of stacked firewood stood in the bare yard, and a weather-beaten barn sagged behind them.

Madame Lefevre was not pleased at sight of the strange big dog her children had brought home.

"Go away, go away!" she ordered, shaking her apron at him from the crude kitchen steps.

"No, Mama, no," cried Fleur-Ange, dropping her lunch pail and seizing the apron with her own hands. "Please let him stay with us. I don't think he has any home."

"We need a dog," put in Joseph with a change of heart after having seen the envy the dog had aroused in the other children. "He's such a big dog."

"That is the trouble," said his mother. "He is too big. He will eat too much."

"He can have part of my food and I won't eat such big helpings," offered Fleur-Ange. "After tonight, that is. I'm so hungry I want all my supper tonight."

"He can have my mush and bread crusts," Joseph offered, adding his bounty to Chalou's diet.

At that moment Grand-père Lefevre appeared at the door, last week's newspaper from Quebec in his hand. He was an old man, bony as a carp and almost as gray.

"What is this about a dog?" he asked, rustling the newspaper.

"The children have brought home this stray dog," explained his daughter-in-law. "We cannot keep it."

Grand-père stepped out the door and peered at Chalou through the thick glasses that magnified his eyes as well as the objects before them.

"This dog must belong to the Montagnais," he said. "They have shaggy beasts."

"May we keep him, Grand-père?" begged Fleur-Ange. "May we keep him, please? The Indians must not want him if they left him behind."

39

"He is too big," put in Madame Lefevre again, although she knew that she was fighting a losing battle.

Grand-père rubbed his chin with his pipe.

"Let them keep him for a while, Corinne," he said to her. "It is lonely with their father away in the lumber camps during the winter and with the fishing fleet in the summer."

Madame grudgingly gave in. "But keep him out of the house," she warned the children. "I won't have him dragging in mud on those big paws. And you, Joseph, don't come in before you take off your boots."

Then Grand-père added another warning. "Do not become too attached to him," he told the children. "You cannot keep him long."

"Why?" asked Fleur-Ange, who was already attached to Chalou.

"He must belong to the Indians," repeated her grandfather. "He will go back to them when they return from their trapping grounds in Labrador."

THE LEFEVRE FAMILY

6

With the Pinard boys Chalou had been a playmate during the winter. The Lefevre children made him a member of their family, and Fleur-Ange rewarded him with many a hug.

That very evening Fleur-Ange and Joseph took him into the house. They did so over their mother's objections. They also did it over Chalou's objections. He balked at the door because he had never been in a house before. Once when he had tried to enter the Pinard farmhouse, Madame Pinard had taken the broom to him. And the new mistress looked ready to do the same.

"He cannot come inside," she objected, barring the way. "His paws are muddy and I mopped the kitchen floor only this afternoon."

41

Joseph righted this by getting an old sack and carefully wiping off each paw. But Chalou held back so stubbornly that Joseph had to pull him by the neck and Fleur-Ange push him by the tail to force him to enter the kitchen.

Madame Lefevre fell back upon a second line of defense. "He can't come in," she insisted although he was already in. "The whole kitchen will smell like a doghouse."

Fleur-Ange thought she could take care of this problem. She went to her bedroom, and reaching up on her bureau, picked the little bottle of violet cologne which she had received as a Christmas present. She had treasured it so dearly that she had never been able to bring herself to open it.

Even now she forced out the stopper regretfully. She lifted the bottle to her nose and drank in whiffs of the fragrance with rapture. Moistening her finger, she rubbed it across her woolen blouse. She was more generous with Chalou. She dampened his head, his back, and his tail.

"Now he smells so good that he can sleep in my room tonight," she stated.

"No, no," cried Madame Lefevre. "He is not a house dog."

But she softened at sight of the desolation on Fleur-Ange's face. "I used a fourth of my bottle of cologne on him," the little girl pleaded, "and it is the only perfume I have. Please let him stay with me tonight."

Madame Lefevre relented. "Then just for tonight," she declared, "but he must sleep in the barn afterward. It should be good for something now that the cows are gone."

The village cows had always run loose to forage over the countryside. When the new air strip had been constructed many years before, cattle could no longer be permitted to roam free because they were a hazard to planes. And it was too expensive to buy fodder for them. So their owners had gotten rid of them and turned to canned milk from the store.

All the while that Madame Lefevre was arguing with Fleur-Ange, Grand-père sat in the rocking chair by the stove and pretended to read his latest Quebec newspaper, which was already four days old. There was a twinkle in his eyes and a smile on his lips.

The next morning at breakfast he straightened out his newspaper and frowned at what he read as he ate.

"I see here that the winter has been so cold that wolves have moved close to many settlements," he informed them. "Ha! I remember some years back they sneaked right into the town of Laprairie to raid garbage cans. Imagine that! Only twenty miles from Montreal. I wonder what that noise was I heard on the back porch last night. Probably the wind."

Madame Lefevre dropped her fork. "Wolves!" she cried. "Wolves trying to get into the house."

"That could easily explain it," admitted Grand-père, dropping the paper beside his chair and buttering his pancakes.

"I heard that a whole pack of them dug a den at the end of the Sept Îles airfield," said Joseph, talking excitedly with his mouth full. "A man killed one with a club."

"Close your mouth when you eat," ordered his grandfather. "It probably attacked him. I remember reading about wolves that got inside a settler's cabin in the old days and devoured everyone in the family."

"Heaven help us!" cried Madame. "Wolves at our door and my husband away in the woods!"

Fleur-Ange was not frightened. "We have a big dog to protect us," she put in. "Prince wouldn't let a wolf eat us. That's what I've decided to call him. He's such a noble dog."

"He must sleep in the house every night from now on," declared her mother. "He is the only protection we have until Robert comes home."

She had quite lost her appetite and so rose to clear the table.

Grand-père solemnly winked across it at Fleur-Ange.

Madame scraped all the leftover pancakes into a big bowl and even added a little canned milk. When she set the food down for Chalou, she patted his head affectionately.

"How lucky we are to have such a big dog," she declared.

One day Fleur-Ange was sitting on the floor beside Grand-père's rocking chair stroking Chalou. The dog was stretched out with his head on her lap. She asked her grandfather, "Why do dogs like to be with people? Today I took a walk up to the fishing wharf to see the men painting their boats. Another dog came up to us and wanted to play with Prince, but he just stayed with me. Why wouldn't he rather be with other dogs?"

Grand-père chewed his pipe and drew in on it several times before he answered. Then he said, "In the beginning God created Adam. But seeing him so weak, He created the dog to

45

protect him and work for him. That is why the dog understands man so well and knows his needs."

Joseph corrected him. "Sister Peronne Marie told us in catechism class that the dog was once a wolf," he stated. "We were talking about Noah and all the animals in the ark."

Grand-père mulled this over for a short while. Then he answered, "Sister Peronne Marie is one smart woman, and she knows many things. But she does not know how to pull in a net filled with cod or how to fell a tree. And she has this matter turned around. The wolf was once a dog, but he rebelled against the Good God's order to protect man, so now he is an outlaw. And he and the dog have been bitter enemies ever since.

Madame Lefevre put in, "You haven't heard that wolf around here anymore, have you? I asked at the store but nobody else has been bothered by wolves. They think it was a fox at our back porch."

"Ha!" scoffed Grand-père. "When that wolf sniffed at our steps and smelled Prince, you can bet he curled up his tail and made for the forest again."

Sometimes the children gathered at Grand-père's rocking chair in the evening to hear stories of the old times when he had been a sailor and had sailed many different ships on different coasts.

"And off Labrador there were great white icebergs," he recounted. "Islands of ice, we called them. They were so big that, would you believe it, there were blue lakes on top of them. That was when I was on the sealing ship *Aurora*."

46

Chalou snuffled softly as if he were half asleep.

"Tell us more, Grand-père," begged Joseph impatiently. "Did you see any polar bears?"

"A few," answered his grandfather, "and of course I have seen many little harp seals because they were what the men were hunting. There were nurseries of them back on the ice floes. We could hear them crying like babies when their mothers left them alone."

"Oh, Grand-père," cried Fleur-Ange in distress, "how could you kill the seal babies?"

"I didn't," her grandfather assured her. "I was only a fireman, so that was not my job. And I don't see how the others were able to kill those young seals. They were like fat little kittens with their fluffy white fur and black noses."

Joseph was always excited by Grand-père's stories.

"I'm going to sea when I get out of school," he declared. "I'm going to sail up the coast of Labrador and see the icebergs and the polar bears and the little seals."

"I'd like to go too," said Fleur-Ange, "but I wouldn't want to hear the poor little seals crying like babies. I don't want animals to be unhappy."

Some days later a May breeze, soft and warm, blew over the village. It brought flocks of the "little white birds"—the arctic buntings—on their way to their nesting grounds far to the north near James Bay. They swirled around the settlements on the north shore like petals of apple blossoms blown from the trees. The sight gladdened the hearts of the Lefevres because they knew that the birds brought spring. And spring brought Papa

Lefevre home from the winter woods. He was a younger copy of Grand-père, with a thin body and strong, wiry arms.

As usual he brought presents for his children—sealskin moccasins trimmed with store rickrack.

"They were made by the Montagnais women in their spare time," Papa explained. "I met some of the Indians coming home from the north. They were portaging their canoes between the rivers."

Fleur-Ange did not look happy as she sat on the rug and slipped the hairy moccasins over her stockinged feet.

"Did they say they had lost a dog," she anxiously asked, "or left one behind?"

"They were too interested in getting back to their own children to talk about dogs," said Papa Lefevre. "They put those of school age in the mission school at Sept Îles while they were away during the winter."

A pang of grief, sharpened by the unfamiliar feeling of jealousy, cut Fleur-Ange. She lowered her head and intently picked at the rickrack on one of the moccasins. For a few moments she didn't say anything, she seemed so absorbed in the moccasin. Then she pushed back her curls and raised her face.

"Now I know why Prince came here," she decided. "He left the grown-up Indians because he wanted to stay with one of their children. And he was looking for that one when he met us on the way to school. We will have to take him back to them, Papa."

THE MONTAGNAIS

7

It was almost forty miles to Mingan—forty miles of a miserable road heaved by the winter freeze and rutted by the spring rains.

Papa was too busy getting his nets ready for the fishing season to drive Fleur-Ange to the Indian camp. And Joseph had been pressed into helping mend the nets. So it was the girl and Grand-père who made the trip—with Chalou, of course.

Madame Lefevre packed a lunch of cold meat pies and tea for them. She waved good-bye.

"I will really miss the dog," she said. "I felt so safe with him in the house when Robert was gone. Perhaps you might get another dog in place of him from the Indians."

"No, no," cried Fleur-Ange. "I don't want another dog."

49

"The Montagnais had some puppies born on the trail," put in Papa. "A soft furry puppy?"

Fleur-Ange hid her face as she leaned over Chalou to scratch his ears. "Maybe," she said.

Then Grand-père climbed into the driver's seat of the old truck. Fleur-Ange ordered Chalou up beside him, then she squeezed into the corner.

She had never gone so far from home. She was eager to see the Indians about whom she had heard so much from her father and her grandfather. Grand-père knew the chief well because they had often met on the river.

"Is he chief because his father was a chief before him?" asked Fleur-Ange, expecting to see a copper-skinned warrior in feathers and furs.

"What a droll idea you have, child," answered Grand-père. "You read too many of those history books in school. A chief of the Montagnais is elected every two years. For almost twenty years it has been that way. And before that I do not believe there were any chiefs because the Montagnais of this shore were nomadic people with only a few families living together along the trap lines. Like in the Lefevre family, the oldest man was the leader." He winked at Fleur-Ange and jabbed Chalou as if the dog could enjoy the joke too. "But you must not tell your papa and mama that," he said to the girl. "I have kept it a secret from them for so many years."

The spruce woods interlaced with tamaracks and birches went by in unending monotony. Pockets of fog sometimes blinded Grand-père.

50

Although he was driving in low gear most of the time, Fleur-Ange would say, "Please don't drive so fast, Grand-père."

And when they came to an open glade beside a stream, she cried, "Oh, Grand-père, let us eat our lunch here even if it is still morning. I want to give Prince some of mine—like I did the first time I ever saw him. Don't you think he'll remember me better if I give him something to eat before we part?"

"I think he will remember you whether you feed him or not," said Grand-père. "But if you want to keep him longer, we shall eat on the way to Mingan instead of the way back."

Fleur-Ange took charge of the lunch basket and scolded Chalou when he nosed at it. "At least you should go back to the Indians with better manners than you had on the road that day," she said.

But she was generous with the meat pies.

"It's so early that I'm not very hungry," she said to Grand-père. "That's why I'm giving Prince most of mine."

When they were back in the truck, Fleur-Ange suggested, "Let's sing that old song 'The Blue Waves' while we're riding along."

"It is too sad," said Grand-père. "Every time we sing it, you weep."

But Fleur-Ange paid no attention to him. In her high, sweet voice she began singing the story of the three little children who disobeyed their parents by playing in a boat on Sunday. They ran up the sail and soon they were carried toward the sea.

In his own thin, high voice, Grand-père sang the words of their parents on shore, begging them to turn back. And between mounting sobs, Fleur-Ange managed to sing the children's boast: *We shall return. We shall return.* Of course their parents and Grand-père and Fleur-Ange knew that they would never return but would drown at sea—because that's the way the song went.

Fleur-Ange's shoulders began to shake and she reached for the handkerchief in her pocket. Grand-père wiped his eyes behind his glasses, one at a time so he could watch the rough road. Chalou had heard the song many times before in the Lefevre kitchen in the evenings, but for some reason he raised his nose and began to howl dismally. It was as if he sensed that he would not return either. So the song ended in sobs and howls instead of the sound of churchbells ringing as in the usual ending.

"You are not crying about the poor children this time," accused Grand-père. "You are crying because you're giving up Prince."

Fleur-Ange stubbornly shook her head. "It's such a sad song that I like to sing it and cry," she said. "There are times when I like to feel sad."

But after they had passed through a street of Mingan and turned toward the river, her attention was taken by the Indian camp. A light mist from the river veiled it, so that the white tents looked ghostly and unreal. Frame houses at one side stood bleak and deserted. But half-finished snowshoes beside a shed and a sealskin hanging on a line attested to the presence of the Indians somewhere nearby.

As the old truck lurched to a stop near the little white church

with its pointed steeple, Fleur-Ange saw that the Montagnais were all gathered on the weather-beaten dock where a cargo boat was tied. Even as she looked, the boat's whistle hoarsely sounded through the dim fog. As it pulled away, the Indians turned back to their camp.

In little groups they walked over the rough, stubbly grass. There were women in bright loose skirts and shapeless jackets with fat curls framing their faces. An old grandmother wore both a beret and a scarf on her head, and a great silver cross hung over her breast. The men's ill-fitting trousers accentuated their short bowed legs. There was an Eskimo-like flatness to the dark faces.

Grand-père quickly found his old friend Chief Piten. Although the leader was even more wrinkled than Grand-père and most of his teeth were gone, his eyes were sharp as those of the wild creatures he hunted.

But Fleur-Ange's interest was in the children—shy little ones clad in the contents of mission boxes. She saw that she would have to make the first move if she wished to gain their friendship.

"I'm Fleur-Ange," she said politely, "and I've brought your dog back."

She turned to Chalou, expecting him to make a dash for one of them. But he only lagged behind.

Suddenly there was a throaty growl and a shaggy black-and-white mongrel rushed at Chalou. Although he was only half of the big dog's size, he sprang at him with hostility and jealousy. Both dogs rolled together in a fury of growling and snapping.

The Indians burst into activity. A boy began yelling in the Algonquin tongue and grabbed the mongrel by the tail. The other Indians shouted and gesticulated wildly. Fleur-Ange desperately pulled at Chalou. An old grandmother, showing remarkable agility for her age, bounded toward a tent for a pail of

54

water to throw on the dogs. The chief grabbed a stout stick and began to belabor the mongrel.

At last the dogs were separated. The mongrel, fenced in by Indian legs, growled insults at Chalou. Chalou returned them.

"We apologize for the bad manners of our dog," said Chief Piten. "If he wasn't such a good trailer, we would have gotten rid of him long ago. It is fortunate that the others are tied up near the canoes."

Grand-père was bewildered. He pointed at Chalou. "But isn't this one of your dogs too?" he asked.

The chief shook his head. "I thought he was your dog," he said. "He came with you, didn't he?"

"Yes," answered Grand-père, "but we brought him back to you. That is, we thought he was one of your dogs lost during the winter."

"He is a fine big dog," admitted Chief Piten, "and we will be pleased to take him if you don't want him any longer. But I have never laid eyes on him before." He turned toward some others. "Do any of you know this dog?" he asked.

There were headshakes and murmurs of "no." The mongrel growled more viciously to prove that he had never met Chalou before either.

All at once the Indians and Grand-père began to laugh. Fleur-Ange joined them with a sob in her throat. She felt as if her heart had sprouted wings. Chalou did not belong to the Montagnais after all. She could keep him in good conscience.

But the Indians, having had their laugh, were no longer interested in dogs. Grand-père and the chief walked off to one

55

of the tents to have a smoke together. The men broke away to resume their work of fashioning canoe ribs or tightening snow-shoe frames. The women returned to domestic tasks, gossiping in their native tongue about the ship's latest visit, for its weekly arrival was an exciting event in their lives.

Only the children were left to stare at Fleur-Ange and her great dog. Their dog snarled, and receiving no rebuke, moved toward Chalou with head lowered and hackles bristling. A boy picked up the club the chief had dropped and began to beat him.

"Don't!" cried Fleur-Ange. "Don't hit your dog. It is cruel, and he is only trying to protect you. He loves you."

Seeing that such conduct had brought condemnation from the pretty visiting girl, the boy dropped the stick and began to fondle the dog.

"What is his name?" asked Fleur-Ange. "My dog is Prince."

The Indian boy looked embarrassed by such a direct question, but he answered shyly, "Napish—'the little boy.' He isn't very big, but he is our best trailer."

Fleur-Ange was immediately interested. "What do you mean?" she asked. "What is a trailer?"

"He smells the trails of the mink and foxes and other fur animals, so our fathers know where to set the traps. Can your dog do that?"

"I—don't know," said Fleur-Ange. "My father doesn't trap. He cuts down trees in the winter and fishes in the good weather."

56

"Does he hunt caribou?" asked another boy. "Our fathers hunt them."

"N-no," admitted Fleur-Ange, "but one time he shot a bear."

"My mother chops wood," said a little girl in a long plaid dress with a beret flattened on top of her short hair. "Can your mother chop wood?"

"She can when Papa is away and Grand-père's rheumatism is bothering him," admitted Fleur-Ange.

The Indian children began to giggle.

"My mother can chop wood when my father is home," boasted one of them.

"Aren't you happy that your parents are home now?" asked Fleur-Ange. "My grandfather told me that you go to the boarding school in Sept Îles when they are away for the winter. My father is gone all winter too, but I am with my mother and grandfather."

Now the Indian children felt more at ease with Fleur-Ange. They clustered closely around her and the little girl fingered her curls.

"Do you twist them on pieces of spruce bark?" she asked. "That is the way my mother makes the curls beside her face. And the spruce makes the hair smell nice."

"No," answered Fleur-Ange, "my hair grows this way naturally."

The little girl, filled with wonderment, pulled a curl by the end then let go. The children giggled again when it sprang back into place.

57

The Indian boy holding the black-and-white dog by a handful of long hair was bored with such feminine talk. He knew that the white girl was interested in dogs as well as curls.

"Would you like to see our puppies?" he asked her. "They're in the shed."

"Oh, I would love to," exclaimed Fleur-Ange, "but first I had better put Prince back in the truck so there will be no more fights."

Chalou was soon safely imprisoned in the cab of the truck. Fleur-Ange and the Indian children left him to go visit the puppies. But the little mongrel did not go with them. He kept circling the truck on stiff legs, daring Chalou to come out and finish the fight.

And Chalou clawed at the window and growled back until the moisture of his breath on the glass veiled the sight of his rude host.

THE WILDERNESS

8

Madame Lefevre was happy to see Chalou back, but she was not happy about another matter. She led Fleur-Ange upstairs to the girl's room one day and pointed at the rug beside her bed.

"Look," she ordered. "Prince is shedding. The rug looks as if it were woven of dog hair. He must sleep in the barn during the warm weather. Besides, the wolves are gone now and your papa is home."

Fleur-Ange knew that it was useless to argue this time because Papa was there to back her mother up. And so he did when the matter was brought up at supper.

"Your mama told me she spent many long winter evenings hooking that rug," he said. "The barn is the proper place for a dog to sleep."

59

Fleur-Ange turned to Grand-père for support, but the old man kept a discreet silence. He refused to be the leader of the family in this affair.

That night the girl took a lantern and led Chalou to the barn. She stamped a comfortable hollow for him in the old dry straw.

"It will really be softer than the rug," she told him, "and I will leave the door open so you can go out whenever you want." She gave him a good-night hug.

Chalou slept badly, but it was not because he was separated from his mistress.

Although no cows had been kept in the barn for many years, a bovine smell still lingered in the straw. It permeated Chalou's long, sensitive nostrils and kept teasing at his memory. It recalled his duty to return to the herd.

From time to time the dog rose and went outside. He circled the house, then returned to the barn to whine softly as he curled up again in the straw. It was almost as if he were back in the Pinard barn and scented some danger for the cattle.

Next day Fleur-Ange noticed a change in him. When she took him with her to dig little cranberry plants up the river, he acted restless and worried. He whined from time to time.

"What is it, Prince?" Fleur-Ange asked him anxiously. "What is the matter?"

He tugged at her skirt, then made little growly sounds as if he were trying to tell her something in human speech. But she could not understand that he was begging her to return with him to the Pinard farm that lay far, far up the river.

60

He seized the cuff of her sweater between his teeth and clung to it.

"Oh, you're afraid that I'll go away and leave you," she guessed. She put her arms around his neck and looked into his eyes. "I only took you back to the Indians because I thought you wanted to go. I'll never take you away again and I'll never leave you, Prince. Never. I promise."

When she turned back toward the beach, he jumped and barked with joy. But when she left it for the dirt road to the house, he lagged behind. Fleur-Ange had to call to him before he bounded to her side.

The following night Chalou did not lie in the hay long. The urge to return to his duty was too strong. He emerged from the barn in the bright moonlight. He trotted to the kitchen steps, then stood there hesitantly. He began to bark.

A window squeaked open.

"Go back to the barn, Prince," commanded Madame Lefevre's sleepy, irritated voice. "You cannot sleep in the house anymore."

The window banged down and all was silent again. Chalou started down the road but twice returned to the steps. Then his dark form slowly loped along the uneven fence and headed for the west.

Once Chalou had crossed the Rivière au Tonnerre at its neck, he faced sixty miles of spiky spruce forests, rocky mountains, turbulent rivers, and hidden lakes.

61

Day after day he pushed his nose through the tangled underbrush and dragged his sore paws over the sharp rocks. The problem of finding food became a difficult one. He was learning the great price that wild animals pay for their freedom; he was nearly always hungry.

In the blur of an early dusk he made for a tall, thickly branched pine and began circling out a bed for the night in the blanket of needles that covered its roots.

Without a sound of warning, a ghostly form swooped from above and combed his back with sharp talons. So silent was the attack that only the breeze fanned by the great barred wings alerted the dog.

Chalou had chosen a tree which sheltered the nest of a pair of great horned owls in a high crotch. The male, seeing Chalou as a threat to the safety of the little owlets, had declared war on the intruder.

The dog lowered his head and cowered in surprise. As the owl made a second glide toward him with talons stiffened for the attack, it broke the silence with a bloodcurdling shriek that would have paralyzed a smaller prey with terror.

Chalou had recovered himself enough to dodge the fresh onslaught. He recognized his attacker as a great bird, and he was aware of the danger of those murderous claws. He growled savagely in reply as he crouched for the next swoop. One of the owl's claws grazed the skin above his eye, and a thin line of blood reddened the short hairs there.

Now Chalou was in full command of his wits. As the owl came at him with greater daring and recklessness, he leaped

aside. Then as the horned head and jabbing claws passed clear of him, he sprang with lightning speed for the short tail. His fangs jerked at the feathers, pulling the owl to earth.

In a flash the dog released the tail and sprang on the owl's back, his great paws forcing him against the ground. His jaws closed on the top of the short neck before the owl could swing the scimitar of his beak around. Quietly Chalou tore the brown feathers apart and hungrily ripped out chunks of warm flesh.

All this while there was only stillness in the tree above. The female owl had cautiously flattened herself over her chicks.

The following day, with fresh strength gained from his meal on the owl, Chalou was more encouraged to try to cross the next barrier of running water.

The rivers of the north shore are not large—most of them are little wider than streams—but they are as swift and savage as snakes. They coil through ravines, leap the cliffs, and hiss their way through rocky chasms. And their waters are as cold as the northern ice from which they spring.

Sometimes Chalou was battered against the rocks and half drowned.

After he had worked out of one river's gorge by following winding gaps in the rock, he found himself in a long stretch of spruce woods. Later he came to a tableland where a forest fire had taken its toll of the greenery. Charred trunks of trees still stood erect, but their needles were gone and their roots buried in black earth. The dog's own paws sank deeply into the blackened dirt and took on a charred look. Even the rocks were black, their lichens burned to a crisp.

64

When he reached the scorched edges of the burned woods, Chalou was refreshed by moist green vegetation around him once more. But he had the uneasy feeling that he was being followed. It made his hide tingle, and his nose quivered nervously.

A few times he stopped abruptly to sniff, but the wind came from ahead and bore no tales.

He loped along again, frightened by the eerie presence of something unseen and unknown—a ghostly something that was stalking him through the spruce trees.

When he reached a narrow pass between high boulders, he was even more alarmed because he felt that the thing was closer now and perhaps waiting to trap him among the rocks.

So he changed his course, lengthening his route but bringing him across an open plain with rocky outcroppings. It was then that he caught the hostile scent. It was that of wolf. And even as his nose warned him, a lithe gray shape broke from the trees and came after him.

The timber wolf ran swiftly and noiselessly. He did not even growl. He came after Chalou with ominous intent, his yellow eyes gleaming like topaz.

Chalou broke the sinister silence. He growled a defensive warning.

The wolf drove against his shoulder with such speed and force that Chalou was thrown off his feet. As the other sprang for his throat, Chalou raked him with powerful hind paws then rolled over quickly and regained his balance while the wolf readied for another charge.

65

Chalou could barely hold his own against the wolf's primitive strength and cunning. Then he saw that his opponent was not alone. Another silent gray form had slipped from the trees. And yet another behind that one.

He was a valiant dog, but he knew when a battle was hopeless. Pitted against three or more wolves he had no chance for survival—despite what Madame Lefevre had expected of him.

Chalou broke from the first wolf and streaked across the plain. He felt that his only hope lay in outracing his attackers. As he thrashed through bushes and scrambled over boulders, he realized that the wolves were faster than he. And they were on familiar ground.

Then it seemed his chance was surely lost because his way was blocked by the churning waters of yet another river. He gave one backward glance and saw his enemy close on his flanks. He saw the other two wolves split company. One moved upriver to cut off his escape and the other angled off below him.

In desperation the dog leaped into the water, although it was the last place he would have chosen for a crossing. It was still churning from rapids above, and rough eddies warned him of hidden rocks. But he had no choice, and if he had to fight the wolves the very treachery of the current might make it his ally.

So he fought his way through the icy torrent, dragged first one way then yanked another by the whirlpools. But the wolves did not follow. They stood on the shore and stared across with hatred and disappointment.

Wolves seldom will take to water in pursuit of their quarry. Grand-père Lefevre might have told the children, "The pure clean water has been blessed by God Himself, and because of this the renegade wolf fears and hates it."

Chalou's heart was a club beating inside his chest. His heavy paws paddled to its measure. A few times he despaired of ever reaching the opposite bank. But the very fact that the wolves had given up the pursuit heartened him and gave him fresh strength.

When he did stagger out of the cold water, he came upon a dead fish that had been cast ashore by the river's fury. Too exhausted to eat it, famished as he was, he lay with his nose beside the fish. He lay panting with closed eyes and dripping coat for many minutes.

When his strength flowed back, he swallowed the fish in two mouthfuls. Then he hurried on to put as many miles and rivers between himself and the wolves as possible.

POACHERS

9

Chalou worked deeper and deeper into the wilderness. Days later he was surprised to get a strong odor of man. He followed it on and on, then lost it on a wind-leached ridge.

Beyond the ridge was a sunny slope. The dog slowly ambled up it. As he went along, nose to ground, there was a crash in the bushes and a doe leaped out.

Chalou pointed his ears and watched her light bouncing flight, like that of a feather blown by a breeze. He had not seen such a cowlike creature in a long time. For that matter, he had not seen a single cow in months. He investigated the place from which the doe had come, drinking in her scent with interested wags of his tail.

It was when he pulled himself through a tangle of underbrush that he came face to face with the little calflike animal. It lay cushioned in the weeds with great, startled eyes fastened on him—the eyes of Bichette.

Chalou cautiously sniffed over the frightened fawn's spotted body. He was surprised because the scent was so faint. Bichette as a baby had smelled warm and milky. He could not know that Nature had protected the wild youngling in this way.

There had been the calf that the contrary Guernsey cow had once dropped in the woods when she escaped through a gate that Remi had left open by mistake. It would have taken Ernest Pinard a long time to find that hidden calf if Chalou hadn't smelled it out for him.

The dog sprawled on the weeds beside the fawn and grinned at it. He waited for someone to come to get this strange spotted calf with Bichette's eyes.

At last he jumped up and went searching for that someone in the woods. He had smelled the man smell, so he thought that a farm must be nearby. He struck a deer trail leading through a ravine, and he followed it hopefully.

He suddenly stopped. He lifted his nose and sniffed. The wind had turned and he smelled man again. He hurried his paws along.

Where the ravine dropped to a woodland lake, he came to a windfall of dead branches which almost blocked his way. The logs were carelessly arranged in such fashion that an opening invited him to enter.

He pushed his neck in. There was a strong smell of salt cakes

70

just beyond his reach. It reminded him of those that Ernest Pinard put out in the pasture for the cattle.

Chalou squeezed forward to investigate. Then suddenly something as strong as a bolt of lightning struck his neck and tightened around it. In the same instant a terrific force jerked him into the air. Chalou had blundered into a deer snare.

He hung high, snapping his jaws and kicking his hind legs while his forepaws clawed the air. He swung from side to side, trying to free his neck from the iron grip.

There was a crash of undergrowth as a man jumped out of a clump of bushes nearby.

"Come!" he shouted to someone behind him. "We've got her this time."

He was a heavy-shouldered man under his bulging leather jacket. Sandy hair bristled low on his forehead. As he came running to the logs he was followed by a companion.

"I'm coming, Bingo," cried the one in back, a rangy fellow with pale blue eyes beneath a cap worn backward.

By the time they reached the snare, Chalou's struggles were growing weaker.

The man called Bingo stopped under the snare and a curse escaped his thick lips. "It's a dog," he cried. "The devil take him."

The other shaded his pale eyes to look up.

"The dirty flea bait!" he exclaimed. "Serves him right for robbing us of the doe. Let him hang."

But Bingo had a different idea. Already he was trying to bend the heavy branch that supported the wire snare.

72

"Come give me a hand, stupid," he called.

His companion mumbled his disapproval of saving the dog that had disappointed them and sprung their snare to boot. But he obediently helped Bingo pull the branch down.

Soon Chalou was back on the ground, his neck freed from the wire collar. He lay half dead, his tongue lolling, his eyes glassy, and his hind legs now and then giving convulsive jerks.

The pale-eyed man kicked him savagely. "He's going to die anyhow," he said. "That's what he gets for messing up our snare. I think he frightened the doe away, too."

Both men crouched over Chalou, watching him intently. The dog began to gasp faintly. His eyes slowly brightened. His sides quivered.

"He's going to make it, Roby," said Bingo. "This is it. I figure he's some hunter's dog lost since last season. Look how thin and starved he looks."

Roby jabbed his comrade with good nature. "There are those hunters who only go after deer when it's legal, eh?" he asked. "We don't have to worry about that, do we?"

Bingo ignored his remarks. "I figure this dog might lead us to where that doe is hiding her fawn," he went on.

"How's that going to help?" asked Roby. "We don't dare shoot her and rouse up some nosy game warden. That's what you said."

Bingo looked at him with disgust. "It's not her we're after now, stupid," he explained. "It's the fawn. If the dog leads us to where the doe's holed up, maybe we can beat the brush and find the fawn."

73

Roby smacked his lips. "I can taste that tender meat right now," he declared greedily.

He became solicitous about Chalou. He went back to their hiding place and reappeared with a canteen. He unscrewed the cap and dribbled water into Chalou's mouth.

The dog snapped thirstily at the drops. After a while he shakily rose to his paws.

Roby thumped his shaggy side. "There, old fellow," he said. "You'll be all right. It's just that your new collar was too tight."

He guffawed at his own joke. Then he became serious. "And how's this flea bait going to know what we want him to do?" he asked.

"That is the problem," admitted Bingo, "but we can work on it. Perhaps if we give him a smell of deer, he'll catch on. I got another idea."

He pulled a twist of rope from his belt and let Chalou smell of it. "There must be some of the scent left from that other doe we hung," he said.

It wasn't so much the scent of the rope as Chalou's instinctive worry about the little creature in the forest that made him understand what the poachers wanted. It was his duty to lead the men to the baby animal so that it could be taken to the barn where it belonged.

He yipped excitedly and made little motions to retrace his steps up the ravine so the men would follow.

Bingo was elated. "You see how fast he catches on," he cried. "He's one smart dog and I'm one smart man. You see now why I

74

wanted to pull him down." He tapped his low forehead. "It takes brains to be able to look ahead."

Chalou felt like a herd dog again as he led the poachers to the fawn's refuge. The little spotted animal was still there, and the fear returned to its eyes, although it did not move.

The dog proudly turned around and gave Bingo a triumphant look. He boastfully wagged his tail.

"*Sapristi!*" exclaimed the heavy-shouldered man. "It's the fawn—this easy. Our new dog is worth his weight in mink pelts."

Roby smacked his lips again. "Slit the fawn's throat now," he suggested, "and we'll skin it when we get back to the shack."

Bingo pulled a knife from his belt and lightly played his fingers over the blade.

A warning flashed through Chalou's canine mind. He sensed that the men were not going to take the calf to the barn. They were going to kill it.

As Bingo stepped toward the fawn, the sunlight flashed on the blade of his knife. A low warning growl rumbled through Chalou's fangs.

The poacher stopped stock-still, the knife poised. Chalou's growl grew deeper and more menacing.

"Knife him!" shouted Roby, jumping behind Bingo for safety.

"He's too big," replied the other. "He might tear me to pieces."

Bingo cursed. He waved the knife at Chalou. The dog crouched, but did not retreat. His snarls became more vicious.

"This pig of a dog isn't going let us have the fawn," declared

75

Roby. "If we'd brought the rifle with us like I wanted, we could shoot him."

Bingo's eyes did not stray from the teeth of the snarling dog. "We better go back to the shack and get it," he agreed. "Looks like we'll have to shoot the dog to get the fawn."

When the men faltered, Chalou was sure that the fawn did not belong to them. He lunged at Bingo's leg and his teeth fastened into the man's boot. Then the dog let go and leaped back to dodge the knife's sweep at him.

Both men turned and went running down the deer trail. Chalou stopped long enough to see that the fawn was safe. Then he set out after the poachers, his growls falling upon the sound of their scuffing footsteps.

Bingo gave up hope of outracing the dog and began climbing a tree. Roby was right under him. They ascended high into the branches, then braced themselves against the trunk. Chalou stood looking up at them and growling ominously.

"There's one more chance," said Bingo when he caught his breath. "I've still got my knife and I always was good at throwing it."

He climbed lower and braced himself in a crotch formed by the trunk and a branch. He raised the knife and juggled it for balance. He sighted along its hilt, then gave it a quick spin downward. But his boot slipped at the same time. The knife missed Chalou's chest. But its sharp blade stabbed through his right front paw and pinned it to the earth.

Chalou yelped with pain as he tried to tug away from the knife. His struggle cut it deeper into his paw, bruising the bone.

76

But at last the knife loosened from the ground. The dog pulled it out with his strong teeth. He snarled up at the men with pain and rage.

"So you're smart and look ahead, eh?" Roby taunted his partner. "So you won't let me bring the rifle. So you pull this dog out of the snare. And you cannot even kill him with the knife you throw so well. Who is stupid, I ask you?"

Bingo glowered up at him. "Shut up!" he roared. "Or I'll shake you down to the dog."

Chalou grew tired of holding the men imprisoned in the tree, and the pain in his multilated paw was unbearable. He rose and slowly staggered away on three legs. He returned to check on the fawn, leaving a thin trail of blood behind him.

When he reached the thicket, the fawn was gone. Only the heavy scent of deer told the dog that the mother had come back and had led her little one to safety.

Chalou cried to himself and stopped to bite at his paw from time to time as he limped westward.

In a few days the wound was healing well, but two of the claws were turned inward at such an angle that it was painful for him to step on the paw. And again hunger pinched his belly.

When he reached the crest of a slope overlooking the great gorge of the Moisie River, he yipped excitedly because beneath the open flank of earth lay the tracks of a railroad. He found a place where he could easily snake his way down to the shelf of the roadbed.

There he came upon the carcass of an animal that had been struck by a train during the night. It was so mutilated that only the shreds of spotty yellowish fur showed it to be a lynx. The creature's tragedy was Chalou's good fortune. With his belly

78

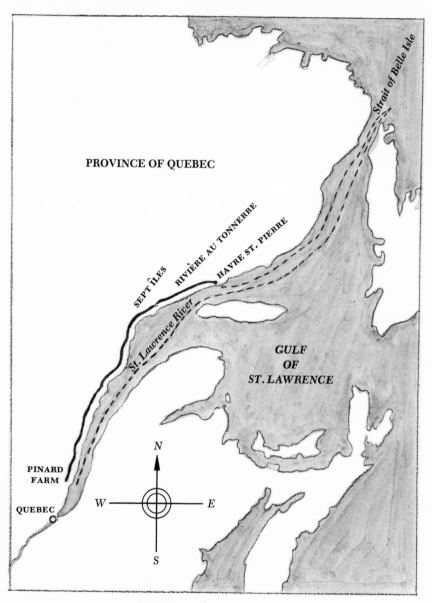

PROVINCE OF QUEBEC

Strait of Belle Isle

SEPT ÎLES

RIVIÈRE AU TONNERRE

HAVRE ST. PIERRE

St. Lawrence River

GULF
OF
ST. LAWRENCE

N

W   E

S

PINARD
FARM

QUEBEC

CHALOU'S JOURNEY

once more filled, he had the courage to limp onward across a trestle bridge and through a dark tunnel.

The tracks led him to Sept Îles, the important ore port on the St. Lawrence River. And from there on, an unending road followed the river hundreds of miles up to the Pinard farm near Quebec. And along the way there would be garbage dumps and handouts at friendly back porches.

HOME AGAIN

10

When Chalou had left the Pinard farm, it was early spring. The cattle were in the barnyard and the fields were covered with snow turned to soft eider by the early thaw.

Now it was summer, and looking ahead, Chalou could see the lush green fields he knew so well and the herd of cattle in the pasture.

He quickened the clumsy steps of his right front paw. The other three moved it along faster and faster. Chalou began to whine in happy anticipation.

There were the fawn-and-white Guernseys with their noses buried in daisies and summer grass. There were rompish new calves playing butting games. And there was Bichette munching near a clump of daisies. Everything was safe and waiting for him.

Chalou scrambled over the wall of giant boulders that formed the eastern boundary of the pasture. He made for Bichette, whimpering his affection.

The Jersey raised her head and looked at him fearfully, the clump of daisies hanging from her horn. She backed up a few steps. He came closer with his ears raised and his nose quivering. Bichette turned and trotted to the other side of the field. From the distance she viewed him with alarm. He pursued her again, and this time she galloped away in fright.

In the months of his absence Bichette had forgotten Chalou.

The dog stubbornly stalked her, trying to force her memory. Then an even more unexpected incident occurred. A powerful dog with blunt white muzzle and short tan hair leaped the rock wall and came at him in a growling fury.

Chalou's first impression was that a strange dog had come to attack the herd. He swerved from Bichette and hobbled to meet the intruder, his fangs bared to the gums. As the strange one leaped at him, Chalou turned aside. The other dog lost his balance and went rolling over in the grass. Chalou was on him, raking his fangs across his shoulder.

As the unfamiliar dog was short-haired, Chalou's teeth cut into the flesh. But the strange dog was all muscle and his legs were strong as iron pistons. He was a descendant of the fierce mastiffs who had guarded the walls of St. Malo in the days of the corsairs.

82

Chalou's long thick hair was protection, but this other dog had equal courage and more stamina. And Chalou was badly hampered by his crippled paw.

Both dogs rushed together with renewed fury. They rose higher and higher on their hind legs until they looked like wrestling bears. But the realization was slowly coming over Chalou that this enemy fought as a dog fights for his own master's property. He was fighting to the death if need be. Accordingly Chalou also realized that the new dog had taken his place on the Pinard farm.

If it had been otherwise, Chalou too would have willingly laid down his life for the safety of the cows. But the sure knowledge that he had been supplanted by another weakened his will to win. He was already badly torn about the nose and his crippled paw kept giving way under him.

He broke away from the tan dog and went yelping off to a corner of the pasture. The other dog followed him relentlessly. He would not be satisfied until the invader was out of the pasture and no longer a threat to the cows.

The excited shouts of the Pinard boys came across the field.

"There's a strange big dog in with our cows," cried Remi.

"Yvan has him on the run," shouted Jean. "Good old Yvan!"

Remi seized a stick lying by the rail fence and vaulted across. "Get him, Yvan!" urged Jean. "That's right. Get him good!"

"He's already got him on the run," cried Remi. "Let up, Yvan. He's going away."

Chalou was trying to pull himself back over the boulders, but his strength was gone. He collapsed into a panting bundle of fur. Remi ran over, club raised over his head. Yvan rushed at Chalou again, proud of a victory which had been witnessed by his masters.

A startled cry burst from Remi's throat. "It's Chalou!" he shouted. "It's Chalou come back!" The raised club came down on Yvan's stout withers. "Go away! Go away!" he ordered the tan dog. "This is our Chalou."

84

Abashed by a victory turned into shame, Yvan slunk toward Jean with his tail between his legs.

Jean was too astonished to say anything. Then he too dropped in the grass beside Remi and ran his fingers through Chalou's thick hair.

"He didn't drown in the river after all," exulted Remi. "He came back. I told you he'd come back someday." He scowled at Yvan. "I told you we shouldn't be in such a hurry to get another dog."

As Remi wiped the blood from Chalou's nose with his own handkerchief and Jean patted his heaving sides, the dog slowly regained his strength. He licked at Remi's hand, slobbering over his wrist.

Yvan stood off, mouthing low growls. To him also had come a bitter realization. For some inscrutable reason this trespassing dog had a right to the Pinard property.

At last Chalou was able to stand up. He grinned happily at the boys. He wagged his feathery tail.

"Come, Chalou," urged Remi. "We must go find Papa."

As the dog followed with his limping gait, the boys were full of concern.

"You hurt his paw in the fight," Remi reproached Yvan, who was following closely and trying to muffle his growls.

Remi knelt in the lane and felt Chalou's paw. Then he glowered at Yvan. "Shame on you for hurting poor Chalou's paw," he scolded.

Jean immediately rose to Yvan's defense. "How could he know that Chalou belongs here?" he asked Remi. "He was only doing his duty." He turned and extended his hand to the other dog. "Come, boy," he called. "You're a good watchdog."

Yvan was encouraged. He drew closer to Chalou, growling louder threats. This shaggy dog might be welcomed by his masters, but to him, he was a hated rival.

Ernest Pinard was as amazed as his sons over Chalou's return.

"It is impossible," he kept repeating, "after these months in the river. He should be drowned. It is impossible that he returns this way." He rubbed his chin unbelievingly. "It is impossible, but it has happened, so we will have to accept the fact that we now have two guard dogs. That will make a difficult problem."

At the boys' request he examined Chalou's paw with fingers sensitive to any defect in a farm animal. "He was not hurt in the fight," he said. "The paw has been injured at some time. It has healed crookedly."

Madame Pinard shared their amazement at the dog who had come out of the river. It reminded her of her cousin Maurice's remarkable return from the dead.

"We buried him from the church with one of the biggest funerals ever seen in Ste. Odile," she said. "Anyway, the body taken from the river was given the fine funeral since it had been identified as that of Maurice because of the big copper-toed shoes."

Ernest Pinard chucked her under her dimpled chin. "And a week later who should walk into your aunt's kitchen but that Maurice who had gone off on a trip to Quebec without telling anyone," he said, finishing her story. "You have told us about it dozens of times—maybe more."

The boys laughed as if they had never heard the story, and Chalou barked.

"But this is the second time such a thing has happened in my family," persisted Madame Pinard, "this returning alive from the river." She shook her head sadly. "Poor Maurice! He could not stand the taunts of everyone who had been so respectful at his funeral." She wiped her eyes with her apron at the memory of her cousin's torment. "So he soon left for Quebec again. And he might as well have been buried in the family plot because he never returned."

"Well, I'll be leaving for the gulf shore next week," Remi reminded her. "Please don't bury me while I'm gone."

The mystery of where the dog had been for so long tantalized the family.

"That ice that broke away must have drifted ashore somewhere down the river," reckoned Jean. "If we only knew where, we might be able to find the fishing cabin and pull it out."

"But why didn't he come home right away?" Remi asked because he was impatient with any mystery. "Where has he been staying all this time and who fed him? Where were you, Chalou?" he demanded of the dog over and over.

It was a great mystery. It would provide table conversation for days to come. It would tantalize Remi most.

Remi Leaves Home

11

As surely as a sled dog leader whipped in battle by a rival, Chalou knew that he had lost his job as guardian of the Pinard herd. That night when he started for the barn to bed down with the cows as usual, Yvan drove him away with fierce snarls and bared fangs.

During the daytime he might climb the boulder wall and lay across it, but Yvan would never permit him to come any closer to the cows. And Bichette was no longer interested in him.

"It is too bad that Yvan is so mean to Chalou," complained Jean. "I wish they could be friends."

"Never you mind," boasted Remi. "Chalou will get even with him yet. Wait until he gets stronger on Mama's good food. Right now he is the golden dog. He is gnawing his bone and waiting his chance."

They all knew the story of the gilded dog carved on a tablet set over the door of the old post office. In the early days of New France a merchant had been wronged by an enemy. So he had hung over his doorway the carving of a crouching dog with a bone beneath one paw. And in old French writing there was the inscription, "I am a dog that gnaws a bone. While gnawing it I take my ease. But a time will come, which is not yet, when I shall bite him who now bites me."

"We surely don't want another big dog fight," exclaimed his father in alarm. "One of them might get killed. I have been thinking it would be best to get rid of Chalou. After all, he is so crippled that he would not be much help if thieves tried to steal any of the cattle. But he might make a good watchdog for the Leroys upriver."

"He would only return here if he were so close to the farm," said Remi. "I know what, Papa. Let me take him with me to the gulf when I leave. He would be good company when I am by myself."

"Not a bad idea," agreed his father after some thought. "I am really uneasy having two such fierce big dogs as rivals on this farm."

The whole Pinard family was going to see Remi and Chalou off on the boat.

"We must leave early tomorrow so Remi will not miss it,"

Madame Pinard kept saying over and over. "We must leave right after the cows are milked."

Ernest Pinard said, "If you want, we will get up at midnight and milk the cows so we can get an early start."

And Jean said, "You talk as if we are going to drive him all the way to the gulf, Mama. It will not take more than a couple hours to get to Quebec."

And Remi said, "I want to help with the milking. I want to say to each cow, 'Take a good look at my face because you will never see it again.'"

"Oh, Remi," cried Madame, bursting into tears, "you must not talk that way. Surely you will come to visit us anyhow."

Remi gave her a quick squeeze, "I shall come back to visit you but not the cows. I hereby give them to my little brother." He looked down at Chalou. "That's right, boy, isn't it?" he asked. "We are both finished with cows, aren't we?"

Chalou only wagged his tail. He did not know yet that he was leaving cows for good too. Even next morning when Remi's suitcase was lifted into the back of the car, he didn't know that he was going with the suitcase.

"Now you keep good watch over the farm while we are gone," Ernest Pinard instructed Yvan. "Charles Fortin will come over later to see that all is in order—so don't bite him."

Yvan gave Chalou a sly look and growled softly in his throat. Perhaps he thought that Chalou was being left behind too, and that it would be a proper time to fight their grudge to the finish.

Then Remi jumped into the back seat and whistled for Chalou to follow. Because of the dog's crippled paw, he helped pull him in by his long hair, then eased him up on the seat. Jean jumped in on the other side.

As Ernest Pinard put the key in the ignition, Madame turned anxiously and asked, "Now you are sure you have your ticket with you, Remi?"

The young man patted his jacket. "Right over my heart, Mama," he answered.

Ernest Pinard winked at his sons before he turned the key. "And now, madame," he asked his wife, "do you think we are giving ourselves enough time? Will we make the boat?"

Madame shrugged, "If we don't have a puncture or an accident on the way," she answered.

The car rolled down the lane. Yvan, seeing himself robbed of a final battle with Chalou, ran alongside, snarling fiercely. Chalou jumped on Remi's lap, the better to growl back at Yvan through the open window. So that is the way the two rival dogs parted company. And Bichette, grazing in the south pasture, did not even bother to raise her head.

The Pinards didn't have a puncture or an accident on the road to Quebec. Madame thought the latter quite a miracle— the way some of those people drove their automobiles.

"I am glad that I live on a farm in the country," she said. "Actually, a tractor goes fast enough for me."

They drove down the steep hill to the lower town where they had to make a couple of inquiries before they could find the dock where Remi's cargo ship was tied up.

"I told you it's a good thing we left early," said Madame triumphantly. "You see how long it takes just to find the boat."

But when they finally drove onto the dock where the small coastal ship was loading, a dockworker said in a surly voice, "You people seem in a great hurry, but this boat does not sail for three hours—and not then if all these boxes aren't loaded."

"Perhaps we could drive up into the city and do some sight-seeing as long as we are here," suggested Ernest Pinard. "I should like to see the Plains of Abraham again, and maybe that golden dog over the post office—eh, Chalou?"

"No, no," cried Madame. "We might get in an accident or the boxes may get loaded sooner than this man thinks."

"Do you want me to help load them, Mama?" joked Remi. "Are you that anxious to get rid of me?"

Anyway, he opened the door of the car so Chalou could get out and exercise. Then Madame agreed to drive somewhere nearby for a little snack to pass the time—if they didn't go too far, if they could watch the harbor from a window, if they didn't get into that terrible city traffic and have an accident.

So due to Madame's concern and Ernest Pinard's accurate watch and the quick service in the café, the Pinards had only two hours to wait when they returned. But the waiting was hard on Remi, who had never been a patient one.

He took his suitcase on board and a steward showed him the tiny cabin he would share with someone else. He made arrangements for Chalou, who could sleep on deck.

"It is no problem, my boy," said the purser. "We took two

horses and a crate of chickens to the north shore on our last trip."

Ernest Pinard gave his oldest son a quick kiss on each cheek in the old-fashioned way, then honked his nose into his big handkerchief. "And if things don't work out for you, my son," he said, "you'll always be welcome home."

Jean gravely shook his brother's hand and wished him success. "You will surely come home for Christmas," he said. "I'll have a new cabin ready for the ice fishing."

But Madame Pinard threw her arms around Remi's neck and wept against the collar of his brand-new jacket. "You must take good care of yourself," she sobbed. "Eat well and dress warmly and be sure to write home often. Now you are really sure that you have your ticket?"

Passengers were arriving at the gangway from every direction. Remi looked over his future companions appraisingly. There were a few tourists in sporty clothing with cameras slung around their necks. But most of the men going aboard were in plaid or leather jackets and stout boots, and they already had the look of the wilderness stamped on them.

When Chalou found out that he was to go on the ship with Remi, a strange eagerness came over him. He ran around and around on deck, sniffing the crewmen. He seemed to be looking for someone.

As the ship slowly parted from the dock, he went to the railing on the river side and braced his forepaws against the top rail. He sniffed into the wind and let out a few sharp yips. He was remembering his cruises on the *Frontenac*.

93

Remi was thrilled by the trip also. He quickly became acquainted with a crew of electricians on their way to set up a new plant in the bush—as they called the wilderness.

"There's enough power in those northern rivers to turn the whole world upside down," declared a middle-aged man with a sandy mustache. As the ship sailed past great pylons carrying power lines, he faced Remi. "We've got them up in the bush too, marching like giants across the mountains and rivers. Hey, what's the matter with the dog's paw?"

"I don't know," admitted Remi. "He disappeared for a few months and came home crippled."

"Too bad," said the electrician. "He looks to be such a fine strong dog otherwise."

It turned out that most of the passengers were men who preferred life in the wilderness. There were even four gray-robed nuns on their way to nurse in their order's hospital in a new paper-mill town. They too seemed to have the "bush fever," as one of the men called it.

"This north shore is the coming country," declared a great-shouldered miner returning to Labrador. "Bah! The cities of Quebec are centuries old. They're worn out and their citizens have lost their imagination. What happened to your dog? He limps badly."

"I don't really know," confessed Remi again. "We lost him for a few months and when he turned up, his paw was this way."

"Maybe got caught in a bear trap," suggested the other. "And speaking of bears, they're all moving to the north shore too. Only last week a truck hit one on the main road out of Sept Îles.

And they say that there are wolves right on their airport runway."

Remi quivered with the excitement of it all. He was glad that his mother was not there to hear about the bears and wolves.

The St. Lawrence River was gentle in the summer. The brilliant sunshine made diamonds sparkle on its ripples. Later in the day when the haze thickened, there were mirages of indigo-blue islands linked by cloud causeways. But as the ship sailed toward them, they magically disappeared.

Day after day they stopped at one lonely port after another, unloading an assorted cargo of the necessaries produced in Montreal and Quebec by citizens who had lost their imagination.

As soon as the gangway was laid, Remi would take Chalou for a romp ashore.

At the Clark City wharf near low jagged hills, Remi watched bundles of sulphide pulp being loaded from low flatcars into the hold of a nearby freighter. Chalou sniffed the sharp odor blown from the paper mill and limped along the tracks. He remembered the smell but not the wharf. It was too far from the town itself in which he had scrounged a half-eaten sandwich from the gutter.

They approached Rivière au Tonnerre, dodging the great rocks that lay in its harbor. Before them stretched a bare plain with gaunt houses scattered along dirt roads.

Chalou became restless and excited. He paid little attention to Remi's orders. He seemed ready to leap the railing and swim ashore.

"We'll be here only a short time, so don't go too far away," cautioned one of the crew after the ship was moored to the gray-timbered wharf.

Worried by Chalou's erratic behavior, Remi fastened a stout length of rope around his neck. "I don't want you running off and getting us left behind in this dreary place," he said.

Chalou tugged at the rope in his endeavors to lead Remi down a dirt road. He whined and twisted his head until it seemed likely he would slip out of the noose.

In anger and disgust, Remi took him back to the ship and shut him up in the cabin.

"I don't know what's wrong with him," he told his roommate. "Perhaps he is getting tired of this boat. So am I, but they say we will reach Mingan tomorrow. That is where a friend will meet me with his car. He is courting a girl who lives there."

He returned ashore by himself and trudged around the river cove to get some exercise. He stopped to watch fishermen working at the flakes. At some of the tables freshly caught cod were being split and salted. At others, men were turning over well-dried fish that looked like chunks of driftwood.

A little girl in a faded cotton skirt and bright blue sweater came skipping up, her short curls bobbing with each step. She gave Remi a curious look because she saw that he did not belong in the village. She seemed a very friendly little girl as she said, "Good day, monsieur. Are you off the boat?"

"Yes," answered Remi.

"I live with my grandfather and my mother and my brother," she answered with a smile. "My father is out fishing most of the

96

summer. He is never home very much, so I often come to the flakes and pretend that he is busy here with the other men."

"Then it must be lonely for you," said Remi.

"Sometimes," she admitted. "My brother likes to go off with the other boys. I used to have a dog that played with me, but he ran away. Oh, I don't blame him," she added hastily. "He didn't really belong to me."

"A dog is good company," agreed Remi. "I'm taking mine with me so I won't be so lonely away from my family. He isn't much good for anything because he's crippled."

"What happened to him?" asked the girl.

Remi sighed and rolled his eyes skyward. Here was that same question again. "He caught his paw in a bear trap," he answered.

"Poor dog," said the little girl sadly.

Remi turned on his heel to leave. "It was nice talking to you," he said. "What's your name?"

"Fleur-Ange," answered the girl. She pointed across the flat plain. "I live way down that road in the house with the blue roof near the old barn."

Remi arrived at the gangway just as the crewmen were preparing to haul it up.

"Hey!" he cried. "Don't leave me in this dreary village. I am no fisherman."

He hurried aboard and joined others at the railing to watch the ship's departure. As they pulled away he saw Fleur-Ange standing in the road waving to him. He waved back. It wasn't until they were well downriver he remembered that Chalou was still shut up in his room.

The dog turned reproachful eyes upon him and went limping out on deck as fast as his good legs would take him. He saw that the Rivière au Tonnerre wharf had vanished and in its place moved a wild shoreline of rocky spruce-bonneted headlands. He stood on deck and howled mournfully.

REMI'S DECISION

12

A light mist, gray and fragile as a moth's wing, hung over the Montagnais' tents when the cargo ship drew up to the Mingan wharf.

Remi waited on deck, his suitcase and his dog beside him. Chalou's nose quivered with interest, but he did not act wild and unmanageable as he had done at the last port. Remi's eyes swept the weathered planks and beyond for sight of Fabien and his fine automobile.

There was one car waiting, but it was a truck come for its cargo. And all that Remi could see on the wharf were Indians who had come to watch the ship's arrival. There were boys holding little hand-carved boats with crudely drawn signs of $2 on each one. A stout woman with a scarf tied around her head raised a pair of sealskin mittens in one hand and a paper saying $5 in the other. A little girl waved a tiny pair of moccasins on a string. But they seemed shy and unconcerned about making sales, as if seeing the ship was their main interest.

As Remi crossed the gangway with Chalou going ahead, he noticed a few of the children surge forward. He feared that he might have to buy something to get rid of them. That is the way it was in so many villages along the river.

But they did not accost him. They were interested in Chalou, and he returned that interest. He nosed at their hands and wagged his tail.

The children jabbered in their native tongue. Then a boy holding a boat said to Remi in French, "You are bringing the dog back again. We told them that he does not belong to us."

A little girl with a beret on her short hair squeezed in and began petting Chalou. "Allo, Prince," she said. "Big Prince comes back to see us again."

At first Remi paid little attention to them. He stood and craned his neck, looking for some sight of Fabien. That Fabien! He was probably lingering at the girl's house and paying no attention to the time.

Then he began thinking it odd that the Indian children seemed so familiar with Chalou.

"Do you want to give him to us this time?" asked the boy.

Remi put his hand on the boy's shoulder. "What are you talking about?" he asked. "Have you ever seen this dog before?"

All of them nodded. "It is Prince who came here with the old man and the little girl," said one.

100

"What old man and little girl?" demanded Remi.

The boy hung his head. "I don't know who they were. Our chief knew the old man, but he is in the hospital at Havre St. Pierre now."

"He got a bad cough in the north last winter," put in another child.

"Who is in the hospital?" asked Remi. "The old man or your chief?"

"Chief Piten," answered the boy.

Remi studied them with mounting curiosity.

"When did they bring the dog here?" he asked impatiently.

"It was last spring soon after our parents came back from Labrador," offered an older girl.

Some of the adult Indians came up to see what the conversation was about.

"These children tell me this dog was here before," Remi said to a stocky man with legs bowed from long hours of sitting on them. "They must be mistaken. It was probably some other dog."

The man looked at Chalou. "It was this dog," he pronounced. "I remember that day and the fight between him and one of ours."

"Maybe you are mistaken too," suggested Remi incredulously. It seemed impossible that Chalou could have traveled this far from the Pinard farm.

The Indian drew himself up proudly. "A Montagnais is never mistaken about an animal," he said. "He can look at his pile of pelts and tell you in which trap each was caught."

"Why does he limp now?" put in the little boy. "He didn't limp before."

"I don't know," admitted Remi. "He was carried away on the river early last spring and we never saw him again until this summer. We don't know what happened to him all that time."

The man squatted and took Chalou's twisted paw in his hand. He felt it carefully and thoughtfully for perhaps a full minute. Then he said, "It was cut by a knife at some time."

Remi was becoming more and more excited. Part of the mystery of Chalou's whereabouts during his disappearance was being solved—in this strange, incredible coincidence.

"Who were the people who came with him?" he asked. "Where did they come from?"

No one knew, but the little girl said, "The girl's name was Fleur-Ange. She had curls that were not twisted around spruce bark."

The name tantalized Remi. Fleur-Ange! Where had he heard that name before? It hadn't been long ago either. It had been only yesterday. The little girl in Rivière au Tonnerre had said that her name was Fleur-Ange, and she had short curls. She had mentioned a dog. The dog had run away from her. He could even hear the echo of her exact words in his ears: *I don't blame him. He didn't really belong to me.*

He was so intent, putting together all the parts he had learned of this mystery, that he didn't hear the horn honking beyond him.

Then he began remembering the way Chalou had behaved when their boat had moored at the fishing village. He had been

102

wild to get ashore. He had almost dragged Remi down the dirt road in his eagerness to go somewhere. "I live in that old house with the blue roof," the little girl had said.

The horn honked a tattoo.

"Hey! You, Remi! You going to camp here with the Indians?"

It was Fabien. He was in a big car all right. It was so big and square that it looked thirty years old.

Remi rushed toward him. "Fabien, my dear fellow!" he cried. "It is good to see you again. But I have just made a great discovery."

Fabien ran a comb through his long hair. "Hokay!" he said. "So at last you discover that I'm honking at you. Hurry up or I'll be late at Jeanne's house."

Remi gripped the car door. "How far is it from here to Rivière au Tonnerre?" he asked. "Is there a road?"

"Forty miles or more of the worst road you ever saw," said Fabien. "What's wrong? You leave something on the wharf there?" Then Fabien saw Chalou. "Isn't that your farm dog?" he asked. "What is he doing up here?"

He combed his hair again, looked at himself in the rear view mirror, then gave his head a quick shake so the hair fell over his ears just right.

"We've got another dog now," said Remi, opening the back door for Chalou. He boosted him in, then tossed the suitcase after him.

"It's good you brought him," said Fabien. "The hunting up here is great. Deer, moose, bear, ptarmigan, and anything else you want. He'll be a big help next fall."

103

"The trouble is he has a crippled paw," said Remi doubtfully. "He couldn't run down a toad."

Fabien squirmed around and looked at Chalou appraisingly. "His nose isn't crippled," he said. "As long as he can smell birds and chase them out of the brush, he'd still be a big help. Last year I bagged a six-point buck easy enough, but I could have shot my limit of ptarmigans and partridges if I'd had a dog to flush them."

Remi playfully ran his fingers over Chalou's nose. "You see, old boy," he said, "You're still good for something."

But his mind quickly turned from the hunting to the late developments concerning the dog. He was so confused by them that he did not even notice that the sputtering old car bore no resemblance to the handsome vehicle the other had described in his letters. He sat trying to sort the odds and ends of information that had come to him from the Indians.

He couldn't give up the mystery now. He couldn't spend the rest of his days wondering about the girl Fleur-Ange and the old man and how they had come into possession of Chalou—if it had been the same dog. He couldn't write home "and I am not sure, but it looks like Chalou might have floated all the way to the gulf on the ice."

He made his decision. "Fabien," he said, "I'd just be in your way while you're with Jeanne. Will you let me drive your car to Rivière au Tonnerre? It will only take me a few hours. You know how I drive."

Fabien took one hand off the steering wheel and ran it through his forelock.

104

"My good new car on that road?" he asked. "Jeanne will expect me to take her riding and get her out of the house."

"Please, Fabien," begged Remi. "Remember when your father asked me how the dent got in his fender and I didn't tell him? Remember how I coaxed my brother to help you with your math so you could graduate? Remember that time I lent you my best shirt for the dance because I wasn't going?"

Fabien sank lower in the seat and honked the horn twice to help him make up his mind. "Hokay!" he finally agreed. "There is a nice porch swing at Jeanne's and I'm getting tired of driving. But take it easy with my car. It isn't all paid for yet."

Remi gripped Fabien's arm and squeezed it tightly.

"You are my best friend, Fabien," he declared. "You are an angel."

As the car swerved sharply, Fabien yelled, "Let go my arm or we'll both be angels."

As the big automobile hurtled across potholes and ridges in the road, Chalou became more lively. He rubbed his nose against the glass. He kept changing his position. Twice he leaned over and whined in Remi's ear.

The young man thumped his shoulder. "If only you could talk, Chalou," he said. "You could explain all of this."

Chalou could have told him that this road was very familiar to him. By that fallen tree he had encountered a porcupine and had wisely let him alone, hungry as he was. At that bend ahead he had narrowly missed being struck by a logging truck. And twice later he had passed these same places in the Lefevre truck.

When they headed for the dirt road that led to the wharf in Rivière au Tonnerre, the dog could no longer stay still. He trembled all over as if he were freezing. He eased himself from side to side as if he were cramped.

Remi had found the road easily, and he remembered the exact location of the bleak house with the blue roof. He drove to the side of the road and parked near the potato patch, which was now blue and white with blossoms. When he opened the door to get out, Chalou roughly brushed past him and almost knocked him down. He was not taking any chance on being shut up this time.

The dog rushed to the door of the house. He began clawing at it and barking. It was soon opened by an old man with a pipe in his hand.

"Prince!" he exclaimed. "Is it you or your ghost?" He looked up to see a young man approaching.

"Good day, monsieur," said Remi.

"You found our dog," said the old man. "He has been gone so long that we thought it was for good."

Remi laughed with relief that this had been no wild goose chase.

"Then he *was* your dog," he said.

"Come in," invited Grand-père Lefevre, "and have a cup of tea. Oh, Corinne," he called toward the kitchen. "There is a stranger here with our dog."

"I'm Remi Pinard," answered the caller. "I live near Quebec city but I am on my way to Havre St. Pierre."

Madame Lefevre came hurrying in, hastily pushing back the loose hairs from her perspiring forehead. She was busy canning wild cranberries.

"This is Remi—" Grand-père began. But Madame's first glimpse was of Chalou.

"Prince!" she cried. "Where have you been?" She sounded much like Madame Pinard. "Where did you find him, monsieur? We never expected to see him again. It almost broke my little girl's heart. But do sit down. Here in the rocking chair."

She quickly swept the newspapers from its seat.

"I can't stay," protested Remi. "I—I just came to find out what I could about the dog."

He quickly embarked upon his story. The ice-fishing incident was interrupted by a sturdy little boy who came racing into the house all out of breath.

"I saw a big dog in a car who looked like Prince," he began. He stopped to stare in astonishment at Chalou. "It *was* Prince. Good old Prince! Where have you been all this time?"

"Joseph," reproved his mother, "we have company. Say 'good day' to Monsieur Pinard."

Before Remi could return to the ice fishing, Madame went into her part of the story. "The children brought him in one day after school. They found him on the road. It was a lucky thing because he saved us from wolves last spring."

Joseph, rolling on the floor with Chalou, noticed something

107

amiss. "What's wrong with his paw?" he asked. "His toes are bent."

"I don't know," said Remi. "I thought you might know something about it." He was disappointed. It looked as if the cause of Chalou's crippling would always remain a mystery. But now he could write home: "What do you know? Chalou floated all the way to the gulf on that ice. Isn't it even more remarkable than the way Mama's cousin Maurice returned from the dead?"

"Prince!" cried a high little voice as the door opened again. "Prince! You've come home."

The girl ran to the dog and threw her arms around his neck. She laughed and cried at the same time. When her mother called her attention to the visitor, she saw him through a blur. "Oh, thank you for bringing Prince back," she said to Remi.

The young man squirmed uneasily. He hadn't intended to give Chalou to them. He had made the trip to satisfy his curiosity. There was the hunting next fall. How he'd love to get his limit of game birds! Chalou would be so good at finding them.

The girl flicked back her curls and laughed. "I remember you," she said to Remi. "You were at the flakes yesterday. I thought you had gone on with the ship. I was so sure it was you on deck waving back to me." A worried look came over her face. "Where is *your* dog? Is someone taking care of him? Doesn't he miss you?"

"This is my dog, Fleur-Ange," said Remi quietly.

He sighed and began explaining again about the fishing and how Chalou had been carried away with the cabin. "We thought he was drowned," he ended. "Then when my ship docked at Mingan, the Indians told me he was the same dog you once brought there."

"And his poor paw," said Fleur-Ange. She lifted it slowly and held it against her cheek. "I remember you said it was caught in a bear trap."

Remi flushed. "I only said that because I got tired of answering questions about it," he confessed. "The Indians think it was cut by a knife. Perhap he's got in the way of an ax."

Grand-père Lefevre let out a crackling laugh and slapped his knee. "Now there's a tale for you, Fleur-Ange," he said. "It's even better than the song about the three children who were carried away to sea, because it has a happy ending. Prince did not drown after all."

"His name is Chalou," corrected Remi.

"Cha-lou." Fleur-Ange pronounced the two syllables slowly so that her tongue could savor them. "That's a beautiful name. It's better than Prince." The joy that had flashed over her face disappeared. It was stricken with disappointment as she raised it to Remi. "Then Chalou really belongs to you, doesn't he?" she asked.

Remi drew in his breath and let it out quickly. Oh, *là!* He and Fabien could go hunting without Chalou. He would be satisfied with a six-point buck. The birds didn't really matter.

"Yes," he answered Fleur-Ange, "but I brought him back to you. You may keep him."

Still the girl's face was shadowed. "But he will only leave again and go back to your farm," she reasoned.

109

"No," said Remi. "I'm sure he will stay this time. He found out that his place has been taken by another dog, and he is no longer needed. I believe that he wanted to come back to you."

Chalou began to whine and drag himself around on his belly in a most apologetic way. He was trying to tell Fleur-Ange he was sorry that he had run away from her. He was trying to tell her that it would never, never happen again.